NEVER IF NOT NOW

NEVER IF NOT NOW

A Midsummer Knights
Romance

MADELINE HUNTER

Never if Not Now
A Midsummer Knights Romance

Copyright ©2020 by Madeline Hunter

ISBN: 978-0-9970802-1-6

Book Cover Design: Dar Albert of Wicked Smart Designs
Formatting: Nina Pierce of Seaside Publications
Editing: Quillfire Author Services

One

Zander surveyed the field from the battlements of Rose Citadel. The activity spread out below him might appear chaotic to many an eye, but he saw method amidst the chaos. Pavilions rose on poles, establishing encampments. Horses paced in a large paddock built of timbers. Pennants waved, announcing the identities of knights who had arrived for the tournament.

"There are quite a few late arrivals," he said. "They missed the feast last night and today's parade and early jousts. Word has it the road to York was almost impassible from last week's rain."

"I assumed the legalities would discourage some of them," Lord Yves said. "Apparently not."

"It is a fine way to spend midsummer. Warriors grow restless when the days are long and there are no battles to fight."

"And no spoils to enjoy."

That was the whole of it. The large prize for the tournament's champion had drawn most of these knights. It was the main reason Zander had come. Since the law mostly rested with the lord of the manor, who was going to enforce the prohibition on tournaments if he was hosting the event?

"With such a horde descending, I will double the guard for the curfew in the town," Lord Yves said. "Also to discourage brawls such as we had this morning."

"It will protect the women, at least."

One of Lord Yves's dark eyebrows arched into a peak. "Are you suggesting the knights' honor will not be enough protection?"

They both chuckled, since such niceties did not count for much when fighting raised men's blood and ale dimmed their good sense.

Lord Yves's attention kept turning to some encampments near the river. A circle of pavilions implied men gathered in some alliance. Zander had called Lord Yves to the wall specifically to witness the placement of those tents.

"They may just be old comrades in arms," Lord Yves said.

"Or conspirators making use of your tournament to gather for plotting treason."

"Fitzwarryn sent you to keep an eye on things, no doubt. His time on the northern marches makes him too cautious. His letter to me in late spring urging me to cancel this tournament was presumptuous."

"He intended no insult. He merely sought to suggest that a gathering such as this can turn dangerous fast. Factions may decide to make this a little war of sorts, to engender support for their preferred royal brother." Zander pointed to that circle. "If those are Prince John's men, anyone with sympathies to him will seek them out. It is how trouble starts."

"If they are John's, I assume it will become apparent soon. Perhaps you would be good enough to tell me when it does."

Zander doubted Lord Yves was as ignorant as he claimed. No one knew this man's thinking on the struggle between brothers that occupied the lords and knights. With King Richard out of the realm, and a ransom being raised for him that would burden everyone, Prince John had become bolder. Those loyal to either brother would be on that field. Such a pot of stew often came to a boil.

"I will gladly tell you once I find out myself."

Lord Yves left the wall. Zander remained there, watching the activity below. His own pavilion had been raised by his squires two days ago, but he did not sleep in it. Lord Yves had given him a chamber in the castle, one of the small cells set into the keep's thick walls. Zander himself had not been the person honored by that hospitality, but Zander's lord, Jean Fitzwarryn, who had sent Zander to the tourney as his champion. Also, as Lord Yves had surmised, Lord Jean wanted a man here to observe and report on any intrigues plotted between the feasts and jousts.

He watched a long time. The large field that had become a temporary town. Tents for living, and a marketplace for goods could be seen. A large cloth roof on the far edge covered a temporary tavern. Some distance away, near the river, a forge had been constructed to allow an itinerant armorer to repair arms. Behind it tents housed the whores who offered goods other than mercery and iron.

Something diverted his attention. Over by the river, one of the latecomer's tents had been completed. Two men now unfurled a banner outside it. Crimson cloth caught the breeze. Zander watched the red spot flap, curl, straighten, and curl again. It showed a crimson field with an azure lion rampant.

Its presence surprised him. Sir Hugo of York was here.

Elinor gestured to the edge of the space spanned by the tent. "Put those chests there."

Two townsmen lugged in the chests and dropped them. One turned with his hand out. She gave him one of her precious half pennies. The townspeople were charging high amounts for their labor, and she resented how much had been demanded for simply moving chests off a cart. If this continued, she and her father would be living in a ditch after this madness was done.

She examined her home for the next week. The tent needed mending, and one of the chests looked ready to fall apart after its days on the cart that brought them here.

She had already noticed that many of the visitors to this tournament displayed more wealth than she would ever see for herself. Women in fine gowns strolled down from the castle, their feet in high pattens and their hair adorned with headdresses made with luxurious fabrics. The parade had been earlier in the day, and she guessed it had been an incredible display of everyone's best garments and the knights' full pageantry.

She did not envy the good fortune of the women now passing along toward the lists, but she would rather not be the poorest among them. Bad roads had made them late to arrive, but at least it had caused them to miss that parade, and the grand feast last night at which expensive clothing would have been expected.

She threw open her chest. She held up a blue dress and considered whether she could improve it before the grand feast when the tournament ended. A bit of embroidery inside the long open sleeves might help, and some new lacing on the side, but nothing could mask that the lightweight wool had been well worn over the years.

One by one she checked the contents of the other chests. She removed a crucifix and set it near her father's pallet. An old little painting of the Virgin Mary, brought back from Crusade by her father, went near her own. She set out pots near the tent's flap, so they would be handy for cooking, along with a basket for gathering fuel and also some bladders to collect water from the river.

She removed a simple surcoat from her father's garments and set it aside for mending. When she lifted the lid on the final chest, her blood chilled.

She let the lid crash closed, turned on her heel, and strode from the tent. She spied her father talking to another knight at a camp nearby. He saw her coming, and strode forward to meet her.

"You've got the look of an angel preparing to fight the devil." He spoke jovially as he approached, his strides long but his gait stilted due to his bad leg.

"Devil is the truth of it, since one has taken hold of you," she said. "What possessed you to bring your arms?"

"'Tis a tournament, Elinor."

"I know what it is, just as I know the cost of coming here. When I objected to this journey, you promised feasts and festivities. You did not say that you intended to compete."

"No reason for a knight to go to a tourney and not compete."

Her thinking exactly, and her argument for *not coming*.

"You are thinking about this bad leg. It doesn't bother me much, and I won't be running a race."

No, he'd be fighting with sword and mace against men half his age, none with a limp, or eyes that could no longer read their own names.

Even if her father had not been wounded in battle, even if he had not had his health ruined by months in a damp Frankish donjon, his age alone argued against competing. At two and forty, his strength and stamina had naturally declined.

"You have no horse," she reminded him.

"I intend to get one."

"How? We have very little coin. Barely enough for provisions, especially since everything will be priced too high so the townsmen can pluck the fat chickens that have taken to roost in their field."

"Don't you worry about how. I won't be using the coin you have, either."

"No, you won't." She had accumulated that money by working as a servant, plying her needle for others. They had travelled here with two other knights, both of whom would wear surcoats in the tournament that she had sewn.

At least she had a skill to sell. It had kept them in food and some semblance of honor. It would serve her after her father died, so she would not be destitute. She tried not to be bitter, but she heartily wished her father had not answered the call to defend the Holy Land. Some men made fortunes on Crusade. Others, like Hugo of York, came back to a life diminished beyond recognition.

The world of the tournament had enlivened her father's mood, at least. He now grinned at her. "Once I win a few challenges, there'll be enough money so you don't have to sew again. There will be fat ransoms for the arms and horses I take as the winner in my jousts, enough to live well and make a dowry."

She didn't know whether to laugh, scream or cry. She walked away quickly, so he would not see that the last reaction had won. The mention of a dowry had undone her, and she plunged into their tent.

As the flap fell behind her, she halted in her tracks. The tent had an occupant. A man had entered uninvited. She wiped her tears so she could confront him as a knight's daughter, and not a weeping child.

He stood near her pallet, his back to her. He seemed to be studying something. He was a knight, from the look of his fine green tunic and the breadth of his shoulders.. Tall and strong, and still lean in the way that spoke of youth. A knight in his prime. The kind of warrior who would either hurt or humiliate her father in the days ahead.

"Are you looking for Sir Hugo? He is not fifty paces from here. I should tell you that he will accept no challenges today." Or tomorrow, if she had her way. Or the next day.

"I am not seeking him. I was looking for you, Elinor."

Shock froze her. She knew that voice.

He turned. She just stared.

Memories flew through her mind. Wonderful ones, of girlish joy and childish games. The man in front of her had little left in him of the squire she had once known. The wiry strength had turned hard during their five years apart, and the beautiful face had found angles with maturity. The eyes had not changed at all, though. Blue and fiery. Stars few out of them when he was happy, and flames when he was not.

"Zander," she breathed the word more than spoke it. She stood immobilized, while she relived another life.

Her past had found her at this stupid tournament, making her present all the more sad.

"I am not called that anymore," he said while he watched her reaction. He did not expect a good welcome, but the sight of her brought him joy anyway. A lightness entered his soul while it briefly tasted the innocence of those days again, back when he truly believed in knightly honor and goodness and fighting for just causes. He ignored the soulful pain the nostalgia carried.

"I will try to remember that, Sir Alexander."

He made a face. "That sounds strange coming from you. I think I prefer Zander from your lips."

She came farther into the tent, and noticed that he held the little picture of the Virgin. "It was all he brought back with him," she said. "He said the Frankish lord who held him let him keep it, since it was religious."

"Religion was all we had in common with some of the other crusaders." He set the wooden painting back on the ground near the pallet, where he had found it.

"You should leave. Before he returns, you must go."

"I have heard that he blames me. Do you?"

"I blame all men who think war is a game and an adventure. Or an easy path to wealth."

"That is not why we went. We fought for God." He threw out the answer, doubting she would accept it. Still, it *was* the reason. The purpose. The cause. "God Wills It." They would shout that as they rode into battle. Only after many months did he learn that the Saracens were yelling much the same thing.

Elinor stood a bit taller than he remembered. The pretty girl had grown into a prettier woman. Her chestnut hair carried lustrous lights and her skin was still white as snow. Her dark eyes watched him warily. Perhaps she thought he would behave badly, even in this first reunion. He had kissed her once before he left, in a garden. A sweet kiss, full of the ardor of youth on his part. Her first kiss, he was almost certain.

He'd assumed at the time that she would be married before he returned. She was of age. That he'd wanted her then was not enough reason to stay behind, but it emboldened him to steal that kiss.

If not now, never.

"You at least seem to have done well in the years since I last saw you, heading off to fight with the last king in France, and then joining Richard on his crusade." Her gaze traveled down his tunic to his boots. "You have grown and filled out."

"As have you." The filling out part stretched the bodice of her simple dress. She caught his gaze lingering there, and smiled in spite of herself when he grinned.

"I am in the service of Lord Jean Fitzwarryn. He has lands on the northern marches where he guards the realm against the Scots. It is at most a day's ride from here."

"Did you leave the Crusade when the king did?"

"Shortly before. I did not stay long." Long enough, though. Too long.

"There are some Scots here. I have heard their tongue. I suppose they will challenge you if you are in this border lord's service."

"Probably so."

She had walked back to the tent's entry. She now lifted the flap and glanced out. "He will be back soon. Please go."

He did not want to leave. He wanted to take her down to the river and sit and talk about those innocent days years ago. The concern in her eyes made him give up that intention, for now.

He went to the flap. He looked down at her, and felt her warmth in the air between them. "I will see you again soon, Elinor."

He did not make it a request. That would give her the chance to deny him, and he didn't want to hear that. As he walked away, he calculated how he could change her caution to smiles, however, and also how to avoid telling her that Sir Hugo's woes were all of his own making.

Two

"I'll be needing my crimson surcoat mended."

Elinor's father announced that in early afternoon, while she sat sewing garments brought to her by other knights. Word had spread that Sir Hugo's daughter plied an expert needle and took in work, and several squires had arrived with a variety of clothing in need of a few stitches.

"If you had told me in good time that we were coming here, instead of the day before we left, I could have already done it." She did not look up while she spoke, but kept her attention on her stitches. She worked outside to take advantage of the good light in the sun at the side of their tent.

"You'd have refused, so I'm telling you now that it needs mending."

"Put it on the pile in the basket. I will do it tomorrow."

"I need it for tonight."

"I have promised this mending by early morning. Would you have me sewing long into the night?"

"I wouldn't have you doing that for others at all. It isn't seemly. You aren't a servant."

It was an old argument between them.

He sidled over and looked down at her stitches. "I'm of two minds about it here, though. It still isn't fitting, but it doesn't hurt for knights to know you are a practical woman, with such skill. That is attractive in a wife."

"Is that one of your goals here? To find me a husband? I doubt it will be an appealing match since I am so old and I have no dowry. I won't accept such as would want me, so forget that notion right now."

"You are turning shrewish, Elinor. We won't tell them that. It would discourage even the least among them."

"Oh, Father. Please go away and talk treason with your friends. Allow me to do what I am doing without giving me more worries."

"It is not treason to want what is best for the realm. We are only talking about the conditions present now."

"I have overheard some of it since a few are too loud in their boldness. You are talking about replacing one king with another. That is dangerous."

"There is no plotting being done. No insurrections being planned."

"That is good to know. Now, please, leave me to my labor."

He wandered away, no doubt to continue all that harmless talk. Elinor truly wished they had not come now. Those men in the tents nearby gathered to discuss their preference for Prince John over the absent Richard. They complained loudly about the money being demanded by Queen Eleanor to ransom her son. They sneered about how Richard did not speak English.

It was a short path for a group of men like that to talk themselves into the steps that a king would consider treason for certain.

She prayed her father would have the good sense to walk away when that turn in the conversation came. Whatever his bitterness regarding Richard, whatever he blamed the king for doing or not doing, he would not survive such a war.

"Sir Hugo is here," Zander said.

"I know him. We had some doings when younger," Lord Yves said. "He has a pretty wife. Katherine, I think is her name."

"His tent is in that circle."

Lord Yves absorbed that. They were in the Great Hall, watching while his steward tried to tame the chaos created by his guests' retinues. Zander had dallied to speak to his host while on his way to his camp to prepare for another joust.

"Sir Alexander, you make a good spy. 'Tis a pity you are not available to serve as one for me. Although, under the circumstances, it appears you are doing just that."

"He blames the king's men for his wounds and his capture. He is not friendly to Richard."

Lord Yves appeared not to be listening, for he stayed so quiet. Zander just waited. His host revealed little of his thinking, so he did not expect to be privy to it now. As a lord Yves was the king's man, but lords had risen against their lieges before. Richard himself had rebelled against his father.

Zander was making no wagers on Lord Yves's loyalties. He merely counted on the man not wanting intrigues against the crown to start here at his tournament, and later get blamed on *him*.

"I will invite him to dine here some nights," Lord Yves said. "It will be easier to keep an eye on him that way. There is no room left to invite him to stay here. Dining, however—there is always another spot at my board."

"Two spots. He has brought his daughter with him."

"A comely girl?"

"No longer a girl, but very pretty."

"A widow?"

Zander realized he had no idea. Had Elinor indeed married while her father was gone on Crusade? Was she now back with her father as a widow? Or, something else he had not considered, did she have a husband somewhere, alive and well?

"I don't know."

"I prefer widows myself, but we will invite her too. If she is pretty like you say, I'll seat her at the high table. I will send a page to Sir Hugo with my greetings."

Zander returned to his path out of the castle but found it blocked by Lord Marcus Debar. Lord Marcus held rich lands in Essex and had come to the tournament as Lord Yves's guest of honor. At the feast last night he sat to Lord Yves's right, along with his wife and young daughter.

"I watched your joust this morning," Lord Marcus said. "If they all go like that, you will be the champion."

Zander slid onto a bench across the table from Lord Marcus. "It is early yet, and there are other knights who will be harder to defeat than the one this morning."

"Your words are humble, but I wonder if your pride truly is. After all, none of the others are known as The Devil's Blade."

Zander smiled vaguely at the appellation, although he hated it. Nor had his own comrades in arms stuck it on him. An enemy army had.

Lord Marcus called a page and had another tumbler brought. Zander accepted that he would not be returning to his camp for a while. When a powerful lord demands your attendance, only a fool denied him some time.

They drank and discussed the other jousts, with Lord Marcus sharing his opinions on the skills he had thus far observed. Zander let him talk while taking his measure. Like Yves, Lord Marcus was perhaps forty years in age. Still strong in a wiry way, and tall, he possessed an amiable countenance but shrewd eyes, and his hair showed some gray.

A pause finally came, and Zander began to leave. Lord Marcus made a quelling gesture. Zander sat back down.

"You serve Jean Fitzwarryn, I'm told. Do you have land from him?"

"Some." Not much, but he had not been a household knight long, and it was generous in that light. More importantly, he had the chance to buy more with spoils from war or tournaments like this.

"Are you betrothed?"

Zander shook his head but did not show his surprise. A negotiation had just begun. A most unexpected one.

"My daughter Matilda is here, with my wife and me. She is over there," he tilted his head to the right. "My wife is with her."

Zander recognized the two of them, but in truth it was the mother who drew the eyes of men more than the daughter, who appeared young and timid.

"She looks much as her mother did at that age," Lord Marcus said, almost in reassurance. "I married a pretty girl, but soon had a beautiful wife."

"I assume a pretty dowry came with your pretty bride." Zander almost kicked himself for playing this game. He did not want that girl. His reaction was inexplicable, however, and he knew it.

A good marriage could make a man's fortune and change his life. Knights had to be very practical in finding a wife.

"A handsome dowry, and friendships I would have never had otherwise. That is the goal, is it not?" Lord Marcus leaned in and spoke more bluntly. "My daughter comes with 150 hectares that include a strong keep and productive farms. There is good hunting land there too. And, of course, a purse for her household. It is not far from my manor, and her husband will be welcomed in my home. We are well situated in Essex, and many lords visit. Marshall stays whenever he comes our way."

"With such a dowry, you will have your pick of husbands. Lords equal to you will offer for her. Earls. Barons, at least."

"That is how it should be. I face two problems, however. She is the youngest of four daughters, and the alliances forged in those other marriages makes finding any additional alliance difficult. I must consider not only my own preferences but also those of the families now bound to me through those marriages. There are few matches that won't offend someone." He smiled ruefully. "The world becomes very small very fast when you have four daughters."

"Since it happens that way with kings, I expect it also does with earls. What is the second problem?"

"My wife indulges her, and the girl thinks she should have a say in it. I blame it on all those foolish troubadour songs. Well, why make the child unhappy if it can be avoided? So long as I approve of the man, that is."

"Of course."

"As it happens, at the moment she seems to want you."

Zander just let that sit on the board between them for a while. "You should explain to your wife what you have learned about my fortune," he finally said. "She will change your daughter's mind quickly."

"I wonder. My daughter thinks you are beautiful. The eyes of an angel, she said." He chuckled. "Of course, she did not see the fires of hell in them when you fought that joust this morning, but she will fast learn not to ignite those flames to her misfortune."

Zander swallowed a rash inclination to discourage any further talk of this. Fate had just placed all he ever dreamed of achieving right in front of him. One word, one smile, and Lord Marcus would introduce him to his wife and daughter, and it would be done.

All because a child found him angelic.

Still, he did not want to grab this so fast. Not only because the week was still young, and who knew what else might find its way to him. He wanted to make sure Lord Marcus knew what he was getting in this contract.

"If you have learned about me, you know that I fought with King Henry in France, and later went with King Richard on Crusade."

Lord Marcus heard what was being broached. "I am loyal, if that is your question. However—"

It was all the howevers abroad in the land that were the problem.

"Being of Breton blood, your lord, Jean Fitzwarryn, sees a future with Arthur as king. I am less certain. If something happens to Richard before that boy grows into a man, the lords will turn elsewhere if Richard has not sired a child. It is inevitable. Even Marshall will throw his influence to John. I want to see peaceful transitions. I have no interest in a war on English soil."

It was a good answer, and one that was hard to argue against. Whether Zander could believe it was a true answer was another matter.

"You are a generous father to indulge your daughter's preferences," he said. "I would not want you to have second thoughts later. Perhaps you can raise this again, if it still suits you, after the melee. By then she may have found another knight she finds more beautiful and any agreement we made now would distress her."

14

Lord Marcus did not hear a refusal, so he was not insulted. He smiled in agreement, but then raised an eyebrow. "Do you have a special friendship with Lady Judith? I ask because everyone saw her pursuit of you at the feast last night, and she honored you with her favor at your joust this morning. I am not a priest. I do not care from what well you have been drinking these midsummer nights."

"There is nothing between Lady Judith and me, except fancy dancing on my part to escape her."

Lord Marcus roared with laughter. "You have good wits if you knew to run. She is insatiable and bedded other men freely even while her husband lived. It is said a week in her bower will drain a man of his seed for a year." He stood. "I will continue to contemplate my daughter's future, and we will speak again after the melee. In the meantime, you have my permission to dance with Matilda after the evening feasts."

Elinor donned the blue wool that evening. She fixed those long, gaping sleeves so that the new embroidery showed, and tightened the lacing on the side. She settled her good cinture around her hips and draped a thin veil on her head. At her father's insistence she used one of her coins to hire a wagon to bring them to the castle.

"You should have worn your mother's diadem," her father said, giving her a critical examination as he helped her out of the cart.

"I did not bring it." She had, in truth, but not for wearing. When necessary she pried one of the tiny precious stones out of the gold netting, to sell. Her father knew nothing of that.

Together they walked into the Great Hall.

Her father was as happy as she had seen since he returned from France. Ever since that page arrived with the greetings and invitation to dine with Lord Yves, he hadn't stopped grinning. She was glad for him, truly. She just wished that she did not feel like such a peasant as she followed some very beautiful garments up the stairs.

A large crowd filled the hall. Retainers of the honored lords and knights sat at long tables, joining the castle folk. The high table stretched over twenty arm spans. Among the ladies sitting near its center were two wearing jewels from which the candles drew colored sparks.

A page announced them, but with the din in the hall no one much noticed. She began looking for a board onto which they could squeeze.

Her father touched her arm and subtly pointed. From the center of the high table a man of perhaps forty years, dark of hair and eye, gestured for them to come forward.

"We're to sit at the high table, daughter."

"He can't mean for us to sit up there. He only wants to greet you, I'm sure. You said you knew him."

"We'll see, but I'm thinking he also knows of my reputation forged since those younger days and wants to honor me. I told you we should come to this tourney, and that it would change our fortunes."

Elinor doubted the fortunes part, but she was proud to walk beside her father and be greeted by Lord Yves, who spoke as if he indeed knew her father from years gone by.

He introduced them to a gray-haired man to his right. Lord Marcus eyed them both while he exchanged pleasantries, then turned his attention to the woman beside him. She was Lady Margaret, his wife. A young girl, flame-haired like her mother, sat quietly between them.

"Lady Elinor, you accompany your father alone? Has your husband not joined us too?" Lord Yves asked.

"I have no husband, sir."

"A widow, then?"

"No, sir." How embarrassing to admit this in front of his most important guests.

"It is an oversight that I intend to rectify this week," her father said with a conspiratorial wink.

Elinor's face burned. She would kill her father when she got him back to that tent.

"Ah, a betrothal. Such are the merry happenings at a good tourney," Lord Yves said. "My page will show you your places, and we will talk later."

Her father took her hand ceremoniously and guided her in the shadow of the page, who led them along the wall behind the high table.

"How could you say that?" she hissed lowly.

"He has no woman near him that looks to be his wife or leman," he whispered. "I'll warrant we're sitting up here because he thought you are beautiful."

She looked back at their host. "You are truly mad now. Such a man expects silver and lands from his wife, and more beauty than I have ever had."

They were so busy chatting that she had not noticed nor cared where they were being led. Suddenly, the page turned to her. "If you would sit here, Lady Elinor." He gestured to an empty place. "Sir Hugo, you are down here."

The table had chairs, not mere benches, so Elinor seated herself easily. She looked left to see an older man dressed in priest's robes. Then she looked to her right.

Blue eyes sparkling with humor looked back.

"You!" she exclaimed.

"Me," he said with a smile.

She stretched back and looked down the bodies.

"Where is he?" Zander asked.

"Five places down. He is sure to see you, and I fear that moment."

"He is not so discourteous as to try and harm me here and now," Zander said. "He would never violate hospitality thus."

"Before the meal ends, I will tell him I am unwell and have him leave with me. If you are not in the hall at that time, perhaps—"

"He will see me eventually, Elinor. It cannot be avoided." He lifted his goblet and drank.

Oh, how calmly he spoke. How unconcerned. Elinor imagined her father's face when the two of them met again. Nothing would stop a challenge then. Honor would demand one man issue it, and the other man accept.

Zander leaned in. "Do not allow your worry for him to ruin your meal. It would be a shame if you did not taste the delights the castle cooks can conceive."

"How can you think about delicacies when we both know—"

"I know nothing. Nor do you. If you are thinking to ask me to spend the next week watching my path so I avoid Hugo, know now that it will not happen."

Just then a page set a wooden platter onto the board. Smells wafted to her. Delicious ones. She peered at the various fowl covering that board. Her mouth watered.

Zander speared a hunk of meat with his eating knife and deposited it on her plate. A real plate, made of metal. She glanced to the lower tables and saw that even everyone there had such a disk. How rich was their host that all his guests could eat from plates instead of trenchers? It would take twelve servants all day to wash them. Where did a man gain such wealth?

"It is swan," Zander said.

She removed her knife from her cinture, poked it into the swan meat, and tasted. She closed her eyes in a little sensory swoon at the delicious flavor of sauce and fowl. Savoring every moment, she chewed slowly.

She appeared a woman in ecstasy while she ate. Eyes closed, expression astonished, face transformed. A saint seeing heaven might look like that. A woman well pleasured definitely did. A priest sat to her left, and her sensual moan drew his attention. He flushed and looked away.

The saints did not interest Zander. The image of Elinor naked beneath him, her head thrown back like this, her expression luminous with amazement, took hold instead. Desire started its sly burn, tightening his body. When she finally swallowed, he fed her another morsel so his mind could take her even if his body could not.

Another swallow and she held up her hand. "No more. It is too delicious. Sinfully so." She looked at him. Perhaps she saw what was in him, because she quickly looked away, flustered.

"Have you been much in the town?" she asked.

"I arrived three days ago, so I know it well already." If she wanted to talk about small things, he would let her. He would agree to most anything right now while they fed their normal hunger. As for this special one he harbored now, he could bide his time.

"I am in need of good thread, finely spun and well dyed. Do they have such a merchant? I do not trust the itinerate peddlers on the field."

"There is one place that probably has what you need. I think he has purchased better goods at the fairs in anticipation of the tournament." He told her how to find the shop after passing through the wall. "Are you making a new gown?" She looked lovely in the one she wore, but even his unpracticed eye could tell it was well used.

She picked at the blue fabric. "I am sewing something else. Mending, actually. I do it for coin." She smiled, embarrassed. "It is better than being a washerwoman, no?"

Since she meant it as a joke, he laughed along with her. His thoughts darkened, however. Hugo of York had his daughter working as a servant to others, it seemed.

She had always known him well, and now her sharp gaze read his thoughts. "It helps a little. He was hurt, and can no longer take service with a lord. He serves as a gate guard for Lord Morris, but that does little more than keep us in bread. So I do this to feed us."

"Could he not do something more, to feed you better?"

"He is a knight. Other than his skill at arms, what would he do?"

Zander could think of many things Sir Hugo could do to spare his daughter this lowly labor. Teach arms to youths. Counsel in strategies. If Hugo could not find a position such as old or maimed knights typically secured, there were other ways to earn his family's keep. Hell, he could clean dung out of stables if it came to it.

"It is not seemly for you to take in mending, Elinor. You are a lady born."

"That is what he says." She leaned toward him and spoke lowly, with belligerence in her eyes. Her closeness and her scent sent desire climbing again. "I would rather ply my needle for pay and have stew on the hearth than refuse to lower myself and eat only thin broth." She turned back to her plate. "I am no longer the girl you knew, Zander. My circumstances are different now."

He reached over and took one strand of her hair between his fingers. He slid them down the silken length. "You are very much still the girl I knew, Elinor. And whatever change time has wrought in you, it has done far more in me."

Another platter came. Boar this time. The priest beside her could not be bothered with a knife, but simply tore a hunk of the rich meat off the joint with his hands. Elinor glanced over at that, appalled, before carving neatly and passing the platter on.

They talked about simpler things then. He told her about the borderlands, and how Lord Jean's household knights kept busy fighting skirmishes with Scots looking to steal cattle and horses. "He is a marcher lord, much as there are in the west. He has great power as a result because he is the only law there."

"Is he a good man? If he has such power, I would hope so."

"He is a man, Elinor. Sometimes good, sometimes not. Like most of us."

"True, but… even with the mix, a person is either essentially good or not, don't you think?"

The priest, whose conversation with the woman on his other side had waned, interrupted to agree with her. Elinor and the priest then shared their views on the matter at length. Zander did not mind. Courtesy required they not ignore their tablemates. He turned his own attention to the woman on his right, Lady Judith Tremain. She worked her wiles on him, but half his mind remained on Elinor, and the bits of her conversation that reached his ears.

By the time the meal was ending, Lady Judith had let him know where she slept in the castle and suggested he visit her so they could continue their conversation.

"That was bold." Elinor's voice murmured beside him.

He turned and saw her mouth pursed in disapproval.

"Nor did you decline," she observed.

"A knight is always courteous."

"Was that courtesy? It sounded like a man leaving a door ajar."

He laughed lightly. "You are no longer a girl. By now, you know how these things go."

"How is that?"

He looked into her eyes, amused by her scold. "Sometimes, a man beds the woman he wants, and sometimes, he beds the one who is available."

Elinor wanted to sniff and turn away at Zander's bawdy lesson. Instead she could not take her gaze off him. His own had locked hers in place as if he controlled her will. She discovered a rare exhilaration in being captured.

They remained like that, the connection deepening. She could smell the spring flowers in a garden, and feel lips pressing hers softly at first, then with a startling passion.

"Daughter!" The voice boomed as if from a distance. She vaguely recognized it as her father's. "Alexander! Churl! Coward!"

That jolted her out of her reverie.

Zander looked down the table. Her father stood at his place, glaring in their direction.

"Here we go," Zander muttered.

Her father threw back his chair. He came toward them, eyes blazing and eating knife in hand. Zander merely turned away and drank some ale.

"Daughter, you should have told me you were seated next to this man. I'll not have him turning your head with pretty words when he should not even be alive."

"Father, our host sat me here. I would never insult him by refusing his preferences."

He now towered behind her, his hot gaze boring into the back of Zander's head. "What are you doing here, coward?"

Zander did not look back at him, but his quiet voice carried well

21

enough. "Twice now you have hurled that insult, Sir Hugo. Do not do it again."

"I'll call a dog a dog if I've breath left."

"That is the question, isn't it? Whether you will long have breath left if you insult me further."

The guests near them at the table watched, fascinated. Even those at the nearest spots on a lower table waited while tight silence reigned a few moments. She heard a low whisper, coming from she knew not whom. "The Devil's Blade."

"And do not even think to use that knife," Zander added. "Raise it one inch and I will break your arm."

Her father puffed up his chest. "I've no need to cut you down here. I'll be seeing you on the field, though, and exacting my due."

"Father—"

"Silence, daughter." He grabbed her arm and pulled her to her feet, throwing her chair back much as he had his own. It crashed to the floor behind her. "I'll not have you break bread with him." He looked around at all the eyes watching. He gestured to Zander. "This knight and others left me to die on the field. We were sworn to each other, but when things turned bad, they ran, leaving me behind, wounded, to be taken or killed." He sneered at Zander. "I'm glad you came, Sir Alexander. God has blessed me with your presence here, so I can make you pay for how you wronged me."

With that, her father dragged her away, down the whole high table. They stopped half a moment to thank their host, then she tripped out the door, hanging off her father's firm grip.

Three

Elinor walked toward the castle the next morning. She ignored the attention she garnered from some of the camps that she passed. Her father's outburst towards Sir Alexander had made her famous, and not in a good way. Now everyone waited to see what challenge would be issued, by which knight, and how it would all end.

Not well, she knew. A sick sensation had lodged at the pit of her stomach. It had been there all night, and still plagued her. She hid her dismay, however, and strode forth.

She trusted nothing would happen until she finished mending her father's crimson surcoat. He would want to look his best when he fought for his honor. She needed red thread to do a proper job, and she had none, however. Hopefully, this mercer Zander had mentioned would.

Guards stood at the town gate. A sign announced a curfew beginning at dusk. All visitors not staying at the castle had to depart by then. Lord Yves did not want drunken men fighting in the lanes at night.

She made her way through the town, following the path Zander had given her. It was a town like many others, with narrow lanes and half-timbered buildings. Second levels jutted out over the street, where owners had stolen a few more feet for their homes. Gutters ran down the center of river stone pavements, and a stream of water carried away the waste in them.

The mercer's shop stood near the center of the town, facing the church. It looked to be a fine establishment, with new whitewashing. She entered to find tables and boards covered in fine goods. The long table with fabrics drew her at once.

She touched wools and linens of all qualities and colors. She imagined gowns of her own and mantles.

At the very end of the table two bolts rested, of a material she had never seen in a shop. She fingered one of them, a red with a bit of gold thread weaving through. Her fingertips slid over the fabric easily, and it showed her hand through it. Silk.

"It is beautiful, isn't it?"

She startled and looked over to see Zander five paces away. "Very beautiful. How does this town afford such as this?"

"As I said, this mercer has special goods just for the tournament visitors. There are lords and ladies in the castle who can afford such as this. And of course, Lord Yves himself can."

She set aside the silk. Too rich for her, even if she were going to make a new dress, which she was not. She walked around Zander and approached the mercer.

"I need red thread," she explained. "Crimson."

The man poked around some baskets on shelves along the wall. He set down a little skein of thread, tied with a thin rope. Zander warmed her side and picked it up with his fine fingers. He had a handsome hand, masculine and strong, and somewhat elegant in its proportions. A puckered scar ran along his last finger. She supposed he had other scars now as well. Most knights did.

"Are you here to buy thread too?" she asked.

He shook his head.

"Then why are you here?"

"To see you. I watched from the castle until you left your camp and walked up here."

"Shouldn't you be practicing with your sword or some such thing, to prepare? At the least, my father will challenge you, and others probably will as well."

"You must convince him not to. His tournament days are over. He is not fit for it."

"His honor demands it. His anger does too. When he finally returned to our tent last night, he again told me what happened, only with more detail. I would have used that knife on you myself when I

24

heard it all." She took the thread from him and set down the half penny it cost. "Now I must go. I have sewing to do.

"Wait." He pointed back to the silk. "Can you sew that?"

"Of course. It would take a much finer needle than I have, but I can sew it so well that no one would see the stitches."

"Then I want you to make a veil with it, such as women wear over their hair. I will pay you to do this, of course."

She walked over and lifted the bolt of silk. Its end fluttered down, rippling like water. She set it down on the counter. "You want a veil of crimson silk?"

"It is for a lady I know." He addressed the mercer. "She needs fine needles, and silken thread too."

Two needles appeared, so thin Elinor could barely see them. She lifted one. Steel, not iron. Expensive.

She told the mercer how much silk to cut, and soon she had a little stack of goods. The price, when given, almost made her swoon. Zander plucked the coins from his purse.

Apparently, he had found the woman he wanted to bed.

"I will need it by Thursday," he said. "Take this as payment now."

He held out his palm with some coins. It was too much. Such a veil was a simple thing. She need only finish the edges. She took a few pennies, then tucked the goods in a cloth sack she carried. She wondered if his favored woman would think this a special gift, or if she already possessed so many silk veils that she would not be impressed.

"Then that is settled," he said. "Now, come with me, and we will settle something else." He took her hand and led her out of the shop and toward the church.

She tripped after him, annoyed. "I must return to our camp. I cannot be seen with you or my father—"

"Yes, your father. It is he who we must talk about." He continued walking until he reached the church. He dragged her to the little yard behind it and swung her around, so she landed on a bench with a thump.

Expression firm, mouth tight, he stood above her with his arms folded over his chest. "Had it been anyone but your father last night, he would be dead now. Do you understand that? I do not take such insults from any man. No knight would. We would have met last night, and no one there, not the priest and not Lord Yves, would have stopped it."

"Perhaps you would be the one dead."

He looked to heaven. "Elinor—"

"He would have been fighting for his honor, his life. Such a cause can give a man new strength." She narrowed her eyes on him. "I said that he told me again what happened. Last night he talked of nothing else. I daresay he never slept, as he was so angry at the memories."

"What did he tell you?"

"How he joined the call of king and God and went with Richard and his men to the Holy Land. You were one of them. His comrade in arms, from the same household." She spoke the last with a sneer of disbelief. "He said that in the battle for Acre, you and the others left him behind, wounded, to be killed by the Saracens. It was his good fortune, he thought, to be found by that Frank instead. Only that man saw a way to make a small fortune by demanding money to let him return home."

Flames in his eyes now. She had angered him. She didn't care.

"There are battles you win and those you lose, and we won that one because Richard changed the strategy when our position became weak. It was time to retreat and move elsewhere," he said. "We did not leave him. I had him with me. I was taking his weight on my shoulders because his leg wound meant he could barely walk on his own. He slowed us down, but not a man there thought to leave him."

"He would not lie. If you had him, how did he come to be alone on that field?"

"He broke away from me and turned back. We would not go back with him and could not wait. But we did not abandon him, Elinor."

"I don't believe you. Why would he turn back?"

He just looked down at her. Finally, he said "Perhaps, he wanted to die in God's cause."

Would her father do that? Think martyrdom was preferable to life, if it meant certain salvation? Some men might, but she did not believe her father would. She did not think he went on Crusade to die.

Zander's firm statements, his anger and his manner, led her to doubt what she had learned about that day. Yet her father had been just as firm last night. Furious, in a state worse than she had ever seen before. She had to beg him not to return to the castle and throw down a gauntlet.

Zander stood before her, with that face sculpted by angels, watching her with those astonishing eyes. Either he was lying, or her father was. There was only one side for a daughter to choose in such a circumstance.

She stood. "I will make the veil for your lady, but we will not talk again. My loyalty is to Hugo of York. I am his daughter, and it is he I must believe."

She walked away, head high.

Zander watched the competitions from the castle battlements. He had already jousted twice today, after seeing Elinor in the town. He had dispatched both knights with ease. Others would come tomorrow, both in the main competition and in personal combats.

He had said he would take all private challengers. Three already had declared themselves. They were men who wanted the fame of defeating the crusader known as The Devil's Blade.

One of his competitors this morning had been newly dubbed. He did not keep the young knight's arms and horse, or demand ransom for them. He looked to be a knight with much still to learn, but he had an intensity and strength that would serve him well. It was not that Zander was opposed to the spoils of tournaments, or wars. It was why he was here. He merely preferred not gaining riches from those who could ill afford the cost.

Tomorrow two of the knights he would meet would not find him so generous. They were known supporters of Prince John, and would seek to prove the skill of those on their side. His lord, Jean Fitzwarryn, would expect him to show them the opposite.

His gaze found the tents near the river. He could barely see the knights there, sitting in a circle. Did they share stories of prowess on the field, or encourage boldness in John's name?

Hugo of York would be among them. It was a hell of a way to express displeasure with his king over that battle, and the lies he now believed regarding what had occurred. That Hugo had found a way to change his own memories did not concern Zander. That he had thrown accusations in front of hundreds of people did.

That Hugo now taught those lies to Elinor made his blood run hot.

He should have issued his own challenge then and there, the way he was taught. No knight called another coward without meeting in mortal combat soon after. Yet when he had seen Hugo walking down the high table behind the page, he had seen a man with a limp and graying hair. A man growing old. A knight still, but no longer capable of waging war. A knight who had trained him, when he was a squire and Hugo a knight in Lord Morris's household.

He smiled to himself. No, pity and nostalgia were not the reason why he had only warned the man off. The truth of it was he desired Elinor, and if he killed her father having her would be impossible.

In the far distance, beyond that circle of tents and the forge, a figure moved. It was a woman, carrying a large basket. He could barely see her, but a long dark line hung down her back. It swayed the way a braid of hair might. She aimed for a spot on the riverbank shielded by reeds.

Then another movement caught his attention. Two men followed her. Step for step, they trod the exact same path as she, until she disappeared into the reeds.

Elinor set her basket down with a groan. She should have found a cart to carry this washing. The townsmen who had them for hire had raised the fee today, however. She could ill afford to pay for a cart when she could carry the basket herself.

She pushed the basket through the reeds down to the river. She tied up her skirt to keep it dry. Kneeling, she began to wash. The water sloshed over her bare legs, but she did not mind. The day was hot, and the water cooled her skin.

Pride interfered with doing this closer to their camp. She did not want people to see her, and the reeds afforded privacy. Like everything else, washing could be bought for little money. A penny here, a penny there, however, and soon there would be no coin at all.

Her father insisted their fortunes would change with this tournament. She had assumed he thought to meet in combat, and claim the forfeited arms of those he defeated. Yet no challenges had been issued by him, and none received.

Eventually, she knew, he would challenge Zander, though.

Last evening, while sitting behind their tent in the cool night air, she had overheard her father talking to another of the knights he met with so often. It seemed Zander's lord, this Jean Fitzwarryn, was very much the king's man, and as a marcher lord, powerful in his own right. Zander was here as his representative, so to defeat Zander was to defeat the lord himself. The other knight said Prince John would be pleased when he learned of it.

She puzzled over her father's plans while she washed. It seemed his anger at Zander was not the only reason he wanted to fight him. Gaining Prince John's favor mattered too. That favor, and the life it could bring was, she suspected, what he meant about their fortunes changing.

She smacked some linen against a rock with more force than necessary. She did not think her father would defeat Zander, so the entire journey would prove a waste of time and coin.

Quiet laughter behind her. Men talking. The reeds parted, and two men barged onto the river bank.

They did not appear surprised to see her. They did not look to be knights, but it was hard to know. After all, she did not look like a knight's daughter these days.

"We will stay out of your way," one said. His swarthy face glistened with sweat, and his dark hair hung in dirty strands. "We were told this is a good place to bathe."

His companion, a fair-haired young man, nodded, trying not to grin.

She shrugged and returned to her labor.

Out of the corner of her eye, she saw them discard their garments fifteen feet away. Pale asses agleam in the sunlight, they waded into the river. They splashed and laughed like boys, but whispering also reached her ears.

She turned and laid out some of her washed garments. When she turned back both of them had moved closer to her spot. Only their heads rose above the water, but they both watched her with predatory eyes.

She ignored them, and knelt to wash one of the last linens.

"Are you angry at that shirt? You are giving it quite a beating," the older one said.

She refused to answer. She calculated how long it would take to gather her wet garments and leave.

"I spoke to you, woman. You should not insult me with silence in return."

Alarm prickled her blood. Her isolation, and vulnerability, pressed on her.

"Methinks this servant needs to learn courtesy," the younger one said.

"I am not a servant. I am the daughter of a knight." She cursed inwardly that fear sounded in her voice, but peril now shrieked its warnings through her body.

The older knight stood suddenly, his naked body white where his garments had covered it, but his neck as dark as his face. His cock was engorged, and his eyes dangerous.

She stood too and turned on her heel to run. Splashes behind her said he was after her. She tried to grab a few garments to save them as she aimed for the reeds.

"Walter!" the younger one's voice shouted, but not in condemnation. In warning.

The splashing stopped. She ventured a look back.

Both men were in the water again. The blond one was pointing up-river. Elinor's gaze followed that gesture. There, in the shallows of the river's edge, sat a knight on horseback, watching. Zander.

"The Devil's Blade," the young man murmured.

Zander's horse paced forward a bit, then stopped. He gazed down at the two men. Elinor's breath caught. The fires of hell burned in those eyes.

"Have either of you been to the Holy Land?" His voice carried despite being unnervingly calm.

They looked at each other, astonished, then shook their heads.

"The Saracens have this way of using their swords that is interesting." He withdrew his sword. "They charge, with the sword held out straight from their sides, like this." He extended his arm out straight, with his sword continuing the line into space. "It works like a scythe in removing heads from bodies." He held up his sword and looked at it. "Of course, they have those special swords that are curved and amazingly sharp, and that might make it more merciful. Still, I have always wondered. . ." He looked right at them. "Don't move, and we will see whether I can manage so clean a death for you."

Shock masked their faces. "You've no cause!" the younger one cried.

"There was no denying your intentions with this woman. I not only have cause—I have a duty. I'll be sure there is enough space to get my horse to a gallop. Without enough speed I will make a mess of it, and finishing will be disgusting for all of us." He began backing up his palfrey.

Curses. Splashes. Two white naked bodies, now with very flaccid cocks, scrambled toward the river bank. Not bothering with the garments they had discarded they ran through the mud up the bank, past the drying laundry, and plunged into the reeds.

As she bent to lift one of her linens that their muddy feet had soiled, Zander's horse blurred past her, chasing them.

She knelt and threw the soiled linen back into the water.

"You should not have come here alone."

She turned as the familiar voice sounded right behind her. Zander stood watching her labor, his horse's mane visible on the other side of the reeds.

"It seems not. I thank you for your protection. I am sincerely grateful. However, you should go away. I said we would not talk again." She returned to the linen, handling it more gently.

He came to her and sat in the grass. "We don't have to talk. I'll just watch and make sure no other men decide to save the cost of the whores."

"As you wish." She made a display of wringing out the linen, then smoothing it on the grass to dry. She plucked the last item from the basket.

Time slowed while she washed it. She could not ignore his presence four feet away. It grew awkward having him just sit there and watch her doing this humble chore. A power he possessed made the air between them tremble.

"Shouldn't you be doing something knightly?" she asked. "Winning combats? Practicing for the next one? Inspecting your arms?"

"I have jousted this morning. I am ready for whatever comes next. When it comes."

"Does no one want to fight Sir Alexander de Mandeville in a personal challenge?"

"Several do. Two today. More tomorrow. And of course Sir Hugo, eventually. Everyone is waiting for that one."

"When a man with a cause fights, I expect it is more interesting."

"It isn't that. There is a rumor that someone will die."

His words caught her as she was wringing out the new piece of wash. She froze, the water dripping over her tight hold on the fabric. She watched those drops snake down ever so slowly, as if time became sluggish.

Most tournaments only saw accidental deaths, if any at all. Sometimes, however, when an important personal conflict was being settled, knights met in deadly combat quite deliberately.

"Is Lord Yves permitting that here?" She tried to sound unconcerned.

"If a good reason is presented, he might allow it."

"Perhaps he will decide the reason is not good enough."

"It is a powerful story your father tells, and of course, I have my honor to defend."

A spike of anger stabbed her mind. She turned and threw the wet cloth at him, hitting him in the face. He showed astonishment while she stood and glared at him.

"How casually you say that, as if it does not matter one whit if someone dies or not."

He stood as well and came over to her. "I am issuing no challenges, so it is not my decision to make."

"You must convince Lord Yves not to permit it."

"You must convince your father not to demand such a foolish thing."

She pictured that competition, with her father limping forward in his old arms, facing this younger specimen of knighthood, believing he might actually win against such a man.

She stomped her foot and wiped the tears starting to stream down her cheeks. "If you kill him, I will never forgive you," she yelled. "I will marry a knight better than you are, and he will avenge me." She beat her fist on his chest with each word. "If he doesn't I will bear a son who will do it, when you are old and lame. You can see what it is like then. I will—"

He pulled her to him and gathered her into his arms. "Becalm yourself, Elinor. I have no desire to kill him. I don't even want to fight him."

She broke down because she knew it would not be up to him, but to a man with too much pride and anger and not enough youth and strength.

He held her while she wept for her father, for her life, for the madness of even being here. Eventually, she began to calm, and she noticed the strong arms holding her closely, and the scent of sandalwood in his tunic and the warmth of his body that despite the hot day was welcomed and comforting.

Two fingers lifted her chin. Blue eyes bedazzled her. Then he lowered his head and kissed her—and the reeds turned to flowers and the grass to ivy and she was six and ten again, in a fragrant spring garden.

***

"Do you remember that day on the edge of the moat?" He lounged, stretched out on his side in the grass amidst her drying laundry, propped on one arm. Elinor sat beside him, her scent surrounding him. She no longer cried, at least.

She had permitted that kiss. She had not pulled away or continued to hit him. Now her arms grasped her bent knees while she looked out over the river. A little frown marred her forehead as if she contemplated that kiss more than he wanted her to.

His mention of the moat made her smile. "You jumped in, as I recall."

"You *pushed* me in."

"You boasted so often how you could swim the entire circle of it, that I sought to see you prove it."

That was not why she had done it. He had been teasing her the way youths do with pretty girls. Joking how, when he earned his spurs, she would have to get in line for any kisses, so she should make good use of the advantage of his current favor of her. When he sought to help her do that, and leaned in to steal a quick kiss, he found himself in the murky waters of the moat.

"Getting in was easy," he said. "Getting out was harder. The banks were steep and muddy as I remember."

She giggled. "You looked like a frog when you finally scrambled up. All brown, with the whites of your eyes peering out." She gave his side a little poke. "A tall, lanky, conceited frog."

"I was not conceited."

"You were terribly conceited. I think you believed one day you would be a king."

"If life were just, I would be." When she laughed at that, he joined her.

Her arm was near his face, with the sleeve still rolled up for her washing. He leaned over and brushed his lips against it, tasting the sweat of the day and her labor. She looked down at what he was doing, her gaze cautious. He would have liked that first kiss to beget others, but he could tell she had been confused by it. So, he resisted the urge to lick the skin of her arm, then of her neck, then of all of her after he laid her down.

This was not the day for it, but to his mind that kiss had been the first step of a journey.

"Is Lady Katherine back at your home?" He asked it to keep her from dwelling on whether that journey was a good idea, which he suspected she now did.

"She died a year after all of you left to go to France and fight for King Henry."

He had inadvertently turned the topic back to her father's misadventures. "I am sorry to hear that."

"She liked you. She said you would grow into a handsome, strong man." She glanced at him with a little smile on her lips. "She was right."

He preened like a fool at the compliment, but only because it came from her.

"Stop grinning," she admonished.

He pushed up, so he sat beside her. "Am I grinning? Lord, it appears I am."

She gave him a little smack and laughed. "Still conceited, I see."

"Is it conceit to acknowledge the truth? If I said 'Elinor, you are a woman distinctively fair in your beauty, with hair and eyes the color of midnight and skin the hue of fresh snow,' it would not be conceited for you to agree with me. A looking glass will reveal the truth of it."

She flushed, so much that he wondered if no one ever spoke courteous words to her anymore. A shame, if so. Perhaps Hugo kept all men away from her. He depended on her more than most men would.

"We will find a looking glass if you don't have one," he said, giving her hand a little pat of friendship. "You will see I am right." Then, since she did not object, he left his palm resting on the warmth of her hand.

She did not move her hand. The kiss, almost chaste in its sweet beauty, had caused nostalgia to drench her, and she still dwelled in poignant memories. She wished they were back then, maid and squire, with one foot still in childhood while the other ventured toward grown-up duties. How easy their friendship had been then. How harmless that kiss in the garden had been.

Nothing seemed simple now. Nothing was harmless. Even as she basked in a connection deep and old, she remained alert for someone coming along the river-bank or sounds within the reeds. She did not want talk that would encourage her father in his plans of vengeance against Zander.

"Why do they call you The Devil's Blade?" she asked. "I have heard it several times now. It is an odd name for a crusader. One would expect such a knight to be celebrated as The Angel's Blade, or The Savior's Blade instead."

"The name was not attached to me by other crusaders, but by an enemy army."

"In the Holy Land?"

"Before that." He did not appear inclined to explain. When she waited long enough, he shrugged. "We first landed in Sicily, to right a wrong the king's sister had suffered there when she was widowed. We took Messina. In the battle, once we were inside the wall, I was attacked by three men. I fought them all." He smiled ruefully. "The next thing I know I am being praised by the king. I am also being avoided, and feared, because the enemy has given me that title. Richard said it was because I fought like a man possessed would."

"Do you not mind?"

"No one uses it to my face. At least, no friend does. It followed me, however. And at times I hear it being whispered. It serves a purpose sometimes."

"By making men fear you?"

"That. And by tempting men to challenge me at tournaments like this one. A bit of fame comes to a man who defeats The Devil's Blade."

The more who challenged him, the more he could defeat. Knights often amassed wealth from the forfeitures that tournament victories brought.

She eyed her wash. The sun had dried it fast, and now it stretched atop the grass, the edges fluttering in the light breeze. It was time to go. She held back a few moments more, savoring the feel of his hand on hers.

"How did you get him home?" he asked.

She knew what the question truly asked. *What does your family have left?*

Nothing. A sad answer, but the only honest one.

"We had some land, as you know. Not much, but—I sold it, except for one-half hectare with a cottage, along with most everything else of value. Lord Morris arranged for the silver to be brought to the knight in France who held him. My father returned two months later, so sick that I nursed him for another two months until he could walk. Lord Morris, out of charity, gave him a post at one of the town gates. It pays barely enough to keep us."

"So you began sewing."

"I had always sewed, like most ladies. I just sell my labor now. That is what is different." That reminded her that, among others, she sewed for Zander. A crimson veil. A gift for a lady. Perhaps he courted his future wife at the meals she did not attend now.

Suddenly, her nostalgia felt foolish and childish. Of course, he would be looking for a wife. The right marriage into an important family would change his life all for the better. He possessed enough beauty and strength to catch a good wife if he sought one, which of course he must do.

She pictured him gifting that veil to his lady, and perhaps helping her drape it over her head and fix it in place with a diadem. She could not see the woman's face but Elinor assumed she was attractive enough for Zander's purposes. More importantly, she had a rich dowry, to be certain. Zander would never be so stupid as to marry a poor woman.

"I must go back." She scrambled to her feet and began throwing the laundry into the big basket.

"I will do that. Go into the river and wash. You will not have the chance again soon. I will turn my back and stand guard, so your modesty is not violated."

Bathing would be heavenly. One could only do so much with rags and bowls of water. "You promise that you will not watch?"

"I promise, and I'll make sure no one else does either." To prove his point, he walked into the reeds.

She looked up and down the riverbank to make sure she would not be seen. Then she dropped her dress down her body and entered the water in her chemise, her laundry soap in hand. Once up to her thighs, she lifted the chemise's hem and walked deeper until she submerged her lower body.

The water enlivened her with its cold contrast to the day's heat. She made quick use of the soap on her body and hair, then plunged down to rinse her long locks.

She stood and climbed back out of the river and let her chemise drop. It stuck to her body and legs, but with the heat today it would dry soon. She pulled on her gown and reached for the basket.

"You will not carry it. I will tie it on my horse." Zander spoke from the edge of the reeds. He looked different. Altered somehow. A compelling power came from him, engulfing her. She found it both frightening and wonderful.

She knew the reason for this change. He had lied. He had watched her in the river after all.

"I will carry it," she said, annoyed that he had lied and uncomfortable because that trembling power wanted to move into her.

"No."

"Someone will—"

"Will see a knight helping a woman with a burden too big for her." He lifted the basket, then leaned down and kissed her lips. Fresh joy breezed through her again. "I will only take it as far as the forge. You can return alone if you want, with the basket on your hip."

It was heavy, so she agreed and prayed no one who knew her father would notice them.

On the way here she had walked right through the little encampment where the whores plied their trade. Zander led his horse around it, which she thought very thoughtful of him. Those little tents made her think about herself, though, and him, and what had occurred.

The beauty and magic, even the pleasure of that kiss, seemed far away already.

She looked at him. He smiled back. As they made their way along the river, she wondered if Zander had decided she had become a woman who could be bedded because she was available, while he courted the woman he really wanted.

Four

"Only the Scot might be trouble." Angus offered the opinion while he sat near the tent's entrance polishing Zander's shield. "He's quick and has a little trick where he feints to one side then quickly swings his sword up in an arc to come down the other side."

Zander rested on his pallet, preparing his spirit for the competitions to come this afternoon. A strong body was not enough. One's thoughts must be strong too.

He watched Angus handle the shield. Angus had ten years on Zander, but remained a squire. Had his skills been better, he would have earned his spurs. Most squires became knights, but not all did. Some like Angus spent their lives as squires.

As his name implied, Angus was of Scot blood. Lord Jean Fitzwarryn had fostered him after his mother was found, sick and hungry, outside a farmer's barn one winter with a babe wrapped in her rough shawl. The mother perished, but the babe survived, and Fitzwarryn gave him the name Angus. "He should know who his people are,"Fitzwarryn had said.

Lord Jean never forgot who his own people were. The descendent of Warryn of Brittany, who had come to England with the Conqueror, Fitzwarryn's ancestor had been given lands on the northern marches by King William, since Bretons had long experience with guarding their borders. The family's Breton interests remained alive and well.

"Just watch that Scot," Angus said.

"I heard you." Zander got to his feet and sat on a trunk. He began putting on his mail hauberk.

Angus set aside the shield. "I'll do that."

"You continue with the arms. Send for Harold. He is useless these days, what with chasing girls and learning to drink too much with the other squires."

"Well, that is what tournaments are for, no?" Angus chuckled, then went to the tent opening and called for Harold.

"Hopefully, they are for gaining other knights' forfeits and taking home good coin. What do you know about the other two?"

"They favor Prince John, that much I know. One, Sir Lionel, has his camp over by the river, with that group of knights who all are of a treasonous bent if you ask me. Sir Lionel is in the thick of it, looking for others of like mind. I saw him as they came in, approaching the poorest among them, starting conversations, pointing them to his camp, being all friendly and helpful."

"Is he here with someone at the castle?"

"His lord, you mean? Not that I know, but I've not been overly friendly with the man."

"Learn what you can about him."

Harold arrived then, out of breath, and set about his duties. Zander stood while the sandy-haired lad clad him in his mail and buckled on the plate that protected his shoulders, neck, and shins. He held the surcoat with Jean Fitzwarryn's colors, and draped Zander in the cloth.

Angus stood, and picked up his shield, helmet, and sword. Harold hoisted the lances and banner. Together, they all walked out to the lists.

Elinor worked her new steel needle, plying it through the red silk. What a joy it was to sew with a good tool, sharp and thin, instead of her old iron ones that she had to sharpen almost daily so they did not ruin fabric. This one pulled the red silk thread cleanly, making invisible holes in the weave of the fine, transparent fabric.

The luxury of the silk seduced her whenever she handled it. Even if she had not wanted to do a good job for the sake of her old friendship with Zander, she would never have given less than her best to such a wonderful material. As it was, her tiny, evenly spaced stitches would create a fitting gift to the woman he courted with it.

She worked to the west of the tent, where the sun shone brightly but the strong breeze did not cause the silk to float like a banner. She heard her father's steps near the front. He was coming back from one of those conversations in another nearby tent. She worried about what was being said there, but when she'd asked he'd rebuffed her, telling her to concern herself with women's things.

"Two of us will meet him on the field this afternoon," a voice said. She recognized it as Sir Lionel. She did not care for the man. His face reminded her of a rat, with its long nose and sparse hair above his lip. Even his eyes, small and intense, contributed to the image.

Mostly, she did not like him because their camp was here, out of the way, due to him. When they arrived on that poor, mud-caked cart, Sir Lionel had extended a welcome before anyone else. He knew her father from years ago. Her father had been glad to see a familiar face, and accepted Sir Lionel's offer for them to camp near him.

So now she lived in isolation, instead of among the central camps where other women could be found. And her father sat in a circle outside with the knights congregated here, complaining and getting up to no good.

"You best leave something of him for me to fight," her father said. "I'll not be denied my right to meet him."

Sir Lionel laughed. "Come watch. We will not keep him from being able to fight another day. We will just make it harder for him to do so. Bring him down a bit."

"I don't need him brought down. I don't want anything to cause people to say it wasn't a clean win when I best him."

"Of course, old friend. Don't worry. Your victory will not be compromised. We wouldn't want Prince John to think that."

A long pause had Elinor stretching her ears.

"You think he will want to see me when he learns of it, for certain?"

"Lord Jean is a thorn in his side. Those marcher lords wield great power, and if they stand against him, he will have too much trouble on the border. He will be delighted that you defeated Fitzwarryn's champion." Sir Lionel's voice lowered conspiratorially. "He will offer you service, and you will never again ride anywhere in a cart."

The conversation became muffled then. They must have entered the tent. Elinor eyed the lower edge of the canvas next to her. If she lifted it with her toe—

"Elinor."

She looked up to see her father standing right in front of her.

"I am going to watch the competitions. I will be home for supper well before dusk."

She merely nodded, then returned to her needle. A few more minutes, and she would have to set it aside to cook. Lord Yves had not invited them to more meals. It went without saying that no one would be eating swan tonight.

She was finishing the end of her row of stitches when Sir Lionel passed by on the way to his camp, talking to a man she had not seen before. This friend had wealth and station, from the looks of his long tunic and noble bearing. He also had cunning eyes, the kind that always seemed to be seeking something in whatever they saw. She could not hear what they said, but she heard her father's name mentioned.

They noticed her, and Sir Lionel stopped talking. Murmurs began again once they had passed. When she brought her sewing to the tent flap, she saw them entering Sir Lionel's pavilion.

She set down her sewing and strolled toward the river to wash. On impulse, she turned her path so she passed behind Sir Lionel's tent. She could hear voices as she approached and slowed her steps.

"He will never defeat him," a voice she did not know said. The other man, she assumed.

"He only needs to make a good show. And John only needs to favor him for it. Once he is John's man, he will be useful, I think," Sir Lionel said.

She stopped walking on hearing that. It was much what Lionel had said to her father about competing against Zander. He now seemed to be discussing the same thing with this man.

"Not very useful in a war."

"I am not thinking about a war." Sir Lionel's voice continued, lower, as if in confidence. "He was with Richard on Crusade. He is known to the king. He can get close to him when the king returns to the realm. If he returns, that is."

A long pause. So long that she worried they had become aware of her presence on the other side of the tent wall.

"Would he do it?"

"He is angry and bitter. He is impoverished, and an offer of lands and a title will convince him, like many others. Only Richard thinks he is a friend, unlike the others."

The implications of what she heard chilled her so much that she couldn't move. Only when two women walked toward her, on their own way to the river, did she force herself to leave the back of that tent.

She hoped she misunderstood. If not, Sir Lionel was using her father badly, and had plans that could send Hugo of York to hell.

Five

"Sir Alexander de Mandeville and Sir Lionel of Wiltshire." The marshal announced the combatants and Zander moved to the plot of field on which the competition would take place. A private combat. No horses and lances would be used per Sir Lionel's requested terms.

He had never met Sir Lionel, but he could tell from the way the man wielded his sword that he was not young. Perhaps he had thirty-five years or so. His sword arm might have been strong ten years ago, but time had taken its toll. He set aside the temptation to finish this fast. There was no profit in humiliating the man. He parried and thrust and swung, and put on a good show. He even allowed his opponent a few sword blows to his shield.

Soon, however, the farce could not continue. Watching for treachery after what Angus had said, he swung the blows that brought Sir Lionel to his knees. In battle, the knight would soon be dead or captured. In a tournament, it ended here. Zander stepped back, and the marshal declared him the winner.

Sir Lionel stood and removed his helmet. He glared at Zander while he began unbuckling the bit of plate he wore.

"Keep them," Zander said.

"They are forfeit."

"Keep them." He began walking away.

"Will you insult me by saying my arms are not good enough for you?" Lionel shouted.

Zander turned. "Will you insist I take them, leaving you nothing for the rest of the week?"

Lionel's long nose twitched and his small eyes squinted. "I've more."

"Fine. Your arms and horse are forfeit." On his words, Angus walked to Lionel and helped him strip off the plate. He relieved him of his sword and carried it all over to Zander.

"Not much use for this," he muttered.

"See if his squire comes to ransom it. Demand only what it is worth."

They walked back to his tent. His next combat was soon enough that he did not divest himself of his mail and armor. He sat awkwardly and drank some ale and waited.

The next knight was more of a test. The man was not so old, and he showed quickly that he was more skilled. He was a big man, however, and that was not always a benefit. He fought furiously, which used strength up fast.

Zander played with him a good while, waiting for him to tire. When the signs of exhaustion showed, he executed his own offense and finally made the moves that brought the fellow down. Once again, Angus collected the arms.

The competition had lasted for almost an hour. The final one would be an hour hence, and part of the official jousts. Angus had warned him about the Scot. Just his luck that one would be last.

This time he did remove his armor, so his body could rest better. Angus pressed some cheese on him, and more ale. He could feel his strength returning. He retreated into his thoughts, to prepare his mind as well as his body.

Elinor gave the soup a good stir. It bubbled lowly over the campfire under the canvas awning she had raised to protect her from the sun. Mostly she stirred to give her something to do while she worried over what she had heard in the neighboring tent earlier in the afternoon.

The competitions had continued all day but should be ending soon.

She saw dots on the castle wall, from where some honored guests watched the competitions. Down here, more would be sitting on a stand to the side of the field where the knights jousted.

Thus far, no challenges had arrived at this tent. Hopefully, none would. Unfortunately, that had become the least of her concerns.

Another cheer went up. Elinor debated with herself. She needed to buy some bread. Why not go now, and take the long way there, so she could watch the tournament for a short spell as she made her way? It would at least distract her mind from its feverish wanderings.

Satisfied that the soup would not need her attention for long while, she went into the tent and gathered her hair at her nape, then bound it with a strip of colored cloth. She changed into a green gown. Then she set out.

The camps grew more chaotic as she neared the lists. Peddlers wound among the tents, offering food and provisions that she never saw offered over by the river. She spied a few women but could not tell if they were there to serve their husbands or their masters.

The crowd had grown thick near the lists, and people jostled for good views. She squirmed through the bodies until she was close to the front at the main field, standing in front of the seated guests. A large field in front of her had been divided, and three competitions raged at the same time.

A combat ended, and a winner was declared. The knights left the field, and two others paced their destriers forward. In terms of size and bearing they looked evenly matched.

"Sir Liam of Kinsale and Sir Alexander de Mandeville."

Her attention riveted on the knight wearing a surcoat of yellow and green. That one was Zander, she was sure.

She did not want to watch. She could not *not* watch.

The Scot was good, Zander had to give him that. After two passes with lances, they met on foot. They parried and thrust and swung, each trying to land a blow that would make a difference. So far, the only difference was that neither one looked to win soon, and the afternoon was passing.

They stood north to south, each of them positioned now in front of a crowd that watched. The onlookers did not like that since none of them could see all of the moves, but neither Zander nor the Scot wanted to have the descending sun in their eyes.

The Scot retreated ten paces and lowered his sword. Zander made good use of the respite to catch his breath. His two earlier combats were affecting his stamina now. It had perhaps been a mistake to announce he would take all challenges since this was the only one that mattered when it came to the champion's prize.

The crowd shouted for the battle to resume. His gaze swept them, halted, then swung back. Dark eyes looked out from behind a man's shoulder.

Elinor was here.

Memories of that kiss this midday distracted him for a moment. Battles have been lost for less. He did not see the Scot's charge soon enough. The man came, sword raised, with an incomprehensible yell bursting from his mouth.

Zander moved, expecting the trick Angus had warned of, waiting for that weapon to make an arc and attack his right side and sword arm. Instead it swung to Zander's left. Just in time, he moved his shield, but a sharp pain said the blade had slammed into the mail on his upper arm. The blade might be blunted, but it still had force. The shock of the blow caused his shield to fall.

Mind bloody with rage, he charged at the Scot without a shield, swinging his sword with both hands and arms. A roar came from the crowd along with some screams. In a dark blur of fury, he slashed and thrust and forced the Scot back until, with one well-placed blow, he hit the Scot's sword so hard that it went flying.

It was finally over, but not without cost. Angus ran to him and looked down at the wound on his arm. "Blood. The mail did it, not the blade, but it will be hell tomorrow."

Zander walked from the lists, gathering salutes from other knights and cheers from onlookers.

A voice shouted "The Devil's Blade."

He made his way to his tent, closed the flap, and sank onto his pallet.

Angus came over with a clean cloth and a thin knife. "That was quite a combat." He spoke conversationally.

"I was distracted." Angus probably wondered how the Scot had managed this blow. It was the sort of wound an inexperienced knight might suffer.

"She must have been pretty," Angus said.

Zander said nothing to that, least of all that she was pretty enough that he had been plagued by daydreams about her that left him hard and hot.

Angus unbuckled and removed the plate on his shoulder, then pushed the surcoat aside so he could clearly see the left arm. "I was going to bring one of the whores here tonight, so you that could celebrate all these victories, but I'm thinking you won't be fit for such labor now."

"You underestimate me. How bad is it?"

"I'm not saying it won't hurt."

"It always hurts. Any warrior who claims it doesn't is a lying churl. Well, get on with it."

"There's a surgeon here. Do you want to go to his tent?"

"You'll do better. He'd probably kill me."

Angus lifted the knife and began prying the mail out of Zander's arm from where the force of the sword had buried it deep into his skin.

It hurt like a devil's bite. He gritted his teeth but had no hope that this would not end with him screaming. As the pain worsened, his mind turned red with anger, and a few curses erupted from his mouth. Angus just worked on as quickly as he could.

"Done," Angus said, sitting back on his heels. "Mostly."

It was the rest that would be total hell. Zander began steeling himself for it.

A shadow fell over them. A presence entered the tent.

"Move, Harold," Angus snarled. "I'll be needing the light."

"I am not Harold."

The feminine voice made Angus stop his preparations. Zander looked down his body to the tent's opening. Elinor stood there in a green dress, with her hair bound in a long braid.

"Are you badly hurt?" she asked.

"Badly enough."

"Don't be paying him any mind," Angus said. "He's seen far worse, and it wasn't his sword arm anyway."

She came forward and looked down at the pallet. "Should you not remove the mail?"

"We can now," Angus said. He gestured to Zander to sit, then went to work on the rest of the armor.

"I don't understand. How were you wounded if wearing the mail and the weapons are blunted?"

"It protected him as it should," Angus said. "But the force of the blow made the mail itself gouge into him. I've just pried it all out."

Zander swallowed a curse as the mail slipped over his arm.

Elinor dropped to her knees beside him. "You appear very pale."

"I'll be paler yet in a short while. You should leave now. Angus is not done with me."

"Can I help in some way?"

"No."

"Yes," Angus said. "You can give him your bare breast to suck while I burn this wound. He never will bite the wood, like any sensible man. He's too vain about his teeth."

"She isn't a whore, Angus."

"Oh. My apologies, my lady."

"Would a bare breast really help?" She sounded concerned, and quite serious. Zander came close to saying indeed it would, just to see if she would offer one.

"No," he said instead.

"Yes," Angus said. "Anything to get him thinking of other than the pain."

"I don't suppose holding his hand would distract him much."

Zander bent the bad arm over his body, reached for her hand with that one, and grasped it. "Not much, but enough."

Angus rose and walked outside. Zander did not look to see what he was doing. He just gazed into Elinor's eyes and hoped he did not scream like a stuck pig in her presence.

There was a lot of blood on the clothes in front of where Angus had knelt. The fear she had been battling surged when she saw those linens now dyed crimson. It didn't seem fair that a knight could wear armor and lose so much blood.

It had taken her a good while to find his camp. First, she had to dodge her father, who was heading to the tavern with some other men. His path forced her to circle around the crowd. Then she needed to find people who could point her toward this pavilion set in the middle of the encampments.

She knelt close to Zander's hip, with their hands grasped on his stomach. Even thus, wounded and in pain, he looked magnificent. His dark, wavy locks now hung with damp, and his pallor worried her, but his eyes gazed into hers with warmth and humor.

Angus returned and knelt again. Elinor glanced over and almost swooned. He carried a knife by a cloth-wrapped hilt, its blade red hot from time in the fire outside.

"Must you?" she asked, almost crying while she imagined the pain.

"He must," Zander said. "Better a burn than the corruption that might start. Now look me in the eyes, pretty Elinor, so I have visions of heaven and not hell."

She looked deeply in his eyes, and refused to watch Angus. She knew when the knife touched flesh, however. She smelt it, and saw for a second how all the lights in Zander's eyes died, buried in a kind of horror that terrified her. Then the hot flames returned, the angry ones. While the stench from the knife continued, he grabbed her with his right arm and pulled her roughly down to his chest and kissed her hard, furiously. She felt his gritting teeth beneath her lips.

Then it was over. Angus knelt back on his heels. Zander's whole body went slack, and he slowly transformed into the Zander she knew.

Angus gathered the bloody cloths and left the tent, closing the flap behind him. Zander still clutched her hand.

"You were very brave," he said.

"I did nothing."

"You did not get all womanish and weepy, or faint."

"You were the one who was brave."

"You helped that part of it."

"It was all the talk, how you defeated him. He is well known as a great champion. He never loses, it was said."

"From the looks of his arms, he rarely does." He glanced to where plate and arms rested. "I think I will keep them. If he never loses, he has many more."

Light suddenly sliced through the tent's space. "Sir!" a young voice cried.

"Welcome, Harold. Good of you to visit."

"I came as fast as I could, sir."

"Well, it is a long way from those little tents near the river."

Elinor looked over her shoulder to see a youth of perhaps six and ten blushing beneath his sandy hair.

Zander did not look in that direction at all. "Leave us, Harold. Find Angus and see if he needs help washing those cloths."

"Yes, sir."

"And Harold—Don't go catching the pox with one of those whores. I don't want your mother complaining to my lord that I did not guard your soul sufficiently."

"Yes, sir."

The light disappeared, leaving them in the shadows again.

"Perhaps you should guard his soul better," she said. "You all but gave him permission."

He shrugged. "Squires practice at many things."

"Did you? When you left Sir Morris's hall, is that where you went?"

"Never. I was as chaste as the castle priest."

They both laughed since the castle priest had been most unchaste.

He cocked a small grin at her. "Don't you need to return to your father?"

"He is at the tavern and said he would not return until supper. However, you should rest, and I should buy some bread to go with our soup."

He shifted his body over. "Lie beside me until I sleep so I don't dwell on my arm. Before you go, take some of the ham and cheese

Angus bought this morning, so you and your father eat more than soup. It is over there somewhere." He gestured vaguely to the other side of the tent.

"Your arm still pains you, I know, but rest will help." She had burned herself on hot pots and knew that flesh rebelled a long while after. He had suffered much more than a brief singe, too.

She settled next to him on the pallet. "I expect you will have to decline future challenges now."

His eyes had closed. "It was not my sword arm. Tomorrow it will bother me some, but less so the next day."

It had been foolish to hope he would say he was too wounded to compete.

She waited until his breathing told her he slept. She rose to go. Before she left she gazed down at him for a long time. Right now, with slumber softening his face, he looked very much like the squire she had once known.

Six

"I think Sir Hugo and his daughter might enjoy a good meal," Zander mentioned it as casually as he could as if a passing thought had come to him.

Lord Yves glanced over from where he broke his fast. He had sat with Zander in order to inquire after his wound. Zander had made light of it and turned the conversation to the other combats, those past and future. Eventually he had slid over to that encampment near the river and mentioned that yesterday Sir Lionel had been the first challenge he met.

Lord Yves had listened to it all with little reaction, but now he showed interest in this meal Zander tried to procure for father and daughter.

"Odd that you are more interested in feeding them than in learning about the Scots sent by King William. Or are you unaware of them?"

"I am aware of them." He was at least aware of two of them. His opponent yesterday had not been one of them, though.

"I would think Fitzwarryn would want you watching them closely."

"It involves a problem in Northumberland, not near us."

"On the border, all areas are near each other when trouble brews. Now, about your unsubtle attempt to encourage another invitation for Sir Hugo—The man called you a coward twice at the last meal. I do not tolerate fighting in my hall, or within the castle walls, among men in their cups. I am not inclined to invite him again."

Zander had not held out much hope, so he accepted that decision.

"The daughter, however—Ah, I see that is the true guest you want at my board from the look in your eyes. Her father hates you. Better to turn your attention to Lady Judith. She has notable wealth, thanks to a husband who never failed to bleed every war for all it was worth."

"One of your widows, however. I would never be so discourteous to my host."

"She has a taste for young knights. Furthermore, I don't like her nose." Lord Yves stood to go. "There is a tin mine on her land that I would not mind having, but I don't think I can face that nose the rest of my life."

Zander laughed. "It is dark at night, so you wouldn't see it."

"Wives have a habit of putting their noses in your face during the day. I will invite Hugo again, but warn him that another outburst like the last and he will be thrown off my land in the morning."

Zander aimed for the hall's entrance. Outside rain poured down, so he procured an oiled cloth before calling for his palfrey and riding to his camp. He had competitions all day long, and from the looks of it, he would be fighting in mud for hours.

Elinor's father returned to their tent at midday. He looked dirty and tired. He sank heavily onto a stool inside. Elinor was busy stacking some sand sacks at the entrance, to hold out the rivulets of water gathering in puddles on the field. It surprised her when her father called her name.

She went to him, carrying a pail and some rags so he could wash himself. Then she dug in one of her baskets and brought out some of the cheese she had received from Zander the night before. She set it down on a cloth near him. "How did you get like this?"

He washed his hands, then took the cheese and bit. "How do you think?"

"I don't think anything. You leave. You return. I assume you are watching the competitions, but that would make you wet today, not filthy."

"Is that how you think I spend my days here?"

Actually, I fear that you also spend them plotting unspeakable things that will lead you to a horrible death.

She had avoided putting words on the last part of her fear before, but images of what happened after such treason hovered like a specter on her spirit.

"When I leave here, I often go to the practice field. I'm not such a fool as to neglect that."

She glanced at the sword he had removed upon entering the tent. He always wore it, but then most knights did. One never knew when it would be needed.

She gave him a long consideration while he finished eating, then washed the worst of the mud off his face and wiped down his tunic. He had lost some weight, but she thought it had been their poor meals doing that, not hard practice. He appeared younger as a result, and it seemed to her that he had shaved with a fine blade, not only used the pumice stones like he normally did.

"I want you to change your garments into something better," he said. "I've a guest coming soon, and you should not greet him in that old gown."

"What guest?"

"You'll see soon enough."

She did as he bid, but resentfully. All that would happen was she would have two gowns with muddy hems to wash now. After changing, she set out two tumblers, some ale, and the rest of that cheese.

The guest arrived soon after. She almost died when she saw him. It was the man with the cunning eyes who had been talking to Sir Lionel yesterday. His name was Sir Gerwant, and as her father explained with a flourish, he was a member of Prince John's household.

"What did you think of him?" Her father waited all of five minutes after their guest left before asking her that.

"He is a proud man and intends to become even more important than he thinks he is already." She spoke while she washed out the tumblers and eyed the amount of ale that had been drunk. She would have to buy more now.

"He is at that. He is also unmarried at present. His wife died last year."

"How sad."

"I was thinking how fortunate, saints forgive me."

It took her a moment to realize what he meant. "Did you invite him here so he could look me over? Are you mad enough to think I might replace this wife he had?"

"He did not think the notion so mad, especially after he saw you. I could tell."

She laughed while she placed the tumblers back in their chest. "Such a man expects far more than I can bring him. What dowry would you offer?"

Her father did not respond to that. He just sat on that stool, thoughtfully.

She feared what he weighed in his head. There were dowries besides those of coin and land.

"I will not have him, so do not worry much over whether he is interested," she said.

"You will have him if I say so," her father snapped before getting up and leaving the tent.

Not if it requires you to do something dangerous and foolhardy, she thought.

She was still giving him a hard scold in her mind when another visitor arrived. A page, this time, from the castle. Lord Yves was inviting them to dine again but wanted to speak with Hugo of York prior to the feast.

Elinor sat at the back of a chamber in the lord's quarters while her father spoke with Lord Yves. From the lord's severe expression, and her father's chagrin, she assumed he was being either scolded or warned. With Lord Yves angry enough to demand this private meeting to express his displeasure, she wondered at the miracle that once again they had been invited to dine in the Great Hall.

Her father walked toward her. She rose and fell into step with him. "What did he want?"

"It is what he doesn't want, which is trouble inside his home. He commanded me to speak not one word to Sir Alexander tonight or be banished from these lands."

She could tell her father resented being called to task like this. She sympathized, but if it kept rash words from being spoken, she was grateful to Lord Yves.

The meal would make her grateful too. As they walked down from the solar, she could smell the food being cooked out in the kitchen. Wonderful odors wafted through the castle.

"It will vex me, not to remind Alexander of his cowardice and how he will soon pay for it," her father said, proving he did not think about the food.

"He was injured yesterday. Perhaps he can't fight anymore this week."

"He met several men today. And how do you know he was injured?"

"I heard about it while I was buying bread."

"Hardly a wound that would keep a knight from fighting, but with a coward, one never knows."

"Everyone saw the blood. Everyone saw how he charged even after being wounded. If you call him a coward for declining a challenge due to an injury—"

"How do you know about the blood, and how he charged?" He looked over at her suspiciously.

"I told you, many people were talking about it."

"So now you worry he will not be fit for a challenge. Look at me, daughter. Watch me walk with one leg half sideways, like a crab. His wound is nothing in comparison and will be sufficiently healed by morning."

They entered the Great Hall. Everyone was seated, and platters were arriving. A page brought her father to a spot on the lord's left side. He escorted Elinor to one five places down from the lord on his right.

Zander again sat beside her, and Lady Judith again on his right. No priest warmed her left this evening. A knight had that place, one who was very tall and so blond it appeared the sun had kissed his hair. She learned he had come from Norway to compete. His English proved minimal but enough for humorous attempts at conversation. She knew nothing of his language, so all she could do was help him try to find enough English words to express himself.

"He is trying to seduce you." Zander's low voice flowed to her ear while she paused to help herself to some venison.

"I think he is only trying to be friendly and courteous."

"So he can seduce you."

"Is that how knights behave? They use good manners to seduce women?"

"Absolutely."

She turned to him and saw Lady Judith over his shoulder. "Is that why you were deep into friendly conversation with that widow beside you when I sat down?"

"Partly."

He didn't even blush at the admission.

She decided a bit of boldness of her own was in order. "Have you visited that chamber she so generously invited you to?"

Zander leaned back in his chair, which gave her a good view of the widow, and the widow of her. Lady Judith made much of cutting her food but kept sending sidelong glances her way.

"No," Zander finally said, as if he needed time to think about the answer.

"Ah, then you pursue a bigger prize than her."

"I do."

Elinor gazed out over the crowded tables, then down the high one in each direction, seeking pretty eyes that might be watching Zander. "Is she here?"

"Yes."

She spied two girls, not much older than she had been when Zander left Sir Morris's manor. Both had a sweet freshness to them that only youth can impart, and that made any female of that age pretty. One sat with a woman dripping in silver chains. The other was Lord Marcus's red-haired daughter.

A sad, hollow spot opened in her stomach, one that food would not fill. She imagined Zander with either one of those girls, and the handsome couple they would make. She pictured him smiling, and those stars leaping out of his blue eyes.

She stiffened her emotions. She turned to him. "Is your arm feeling better?"

"Much better. The burn needs salve, but I can move it without pain." He moved his elbow up and down to prove it. He favored her with a smile that made her insides flutter. "Your help made all the difference."

She had done nothing to make a difference, but she would take the thanks if it meant being bedazzled by his best smile.

"Thank you for the ham," she said, then immediately felt stupid. Of all things to talk about. "My father appreciated it, even if he did not know from whence it came."

"He could starve for all I care. You, however, should not be reduced to soup and bread. Lord Yves's dog boys eat better than that."

"Perhaps you can ask him to give me work as one, so I can grow fat as I grow old." She said it with a laugh, but he did not join her with the merriment.

They partook of the sweets that followed the savories. Zander did not talk much to her or to Lady Judith. He seemed in a sour mood. A little thoughtful and a little angry if she read his eyes correctly. The Norse tried to engage her in more broken conversation, but she did not encourage him. Now that Zander had mentioned it, this man might well have dishonorable intentions.

Zander leaned far over the board and looked down the line of guests. Toward those girls. A small smile formed and suddenly his flames turned to stars. Good humor etched his face. She wondered which girl was receiving that smile.

She reached for another sweet to bury her hurt pride by indulging her stomach.

Seven

Sir Hugo had fallen asleep. Right at the table, in his chair. He was not the first man to have the effects of wine bring him down before a meal ended, so no one paid him much mind.

It was exactly the development Zander needed. If he spent another hour fending off Lady Judith while Elinor accepted the blandishments of a Norseman who could not even talk, he would be looking for a good fight before the meal had finished. He already contemplated whether he could take down that blond giant if by chance they met with only fists as weapons.

Zander rose and walked down the table in the space behind the chairs. He stopped at Lord Yves's spot and bent to the lord's ear.

"Sir Hugo is snoring away, interfering with that lute player's melody," he said. "I would bring him home, but if he is in his cups, he might start an argument with me."

Lord Yves peered down the line of guests. "First you tell me to invite him, and now you tell me he should go home."

"Who expected him to prefer slumber to good company and good food?"

"I will find someone to take him back, just to make sure he doesn't fall asleep in a ditch."

"Why not ask your guest, that Norse knight?"

"Sir Bjorn?"

"He is so big that he could carry Hugo under one arm if necessary."

Lord Yves's gaze slid over and up to Zander's face. "And the daughter? Lady Elinor? No doubt you have a helpful suggestion regarding her too."

"Why should she suffer because her father can't stay awake when he drinks wine? Let her stay. I will see she gets back in good time."

"I'm sure you will." He sighed. "Why do I think Hugo will want to kill you all the more very soon? Fine, either knights or servants will ensure Hugo gets back to his camp, and you will make sure the daughter follows."

With a spring in his step, Zander returned to his chair. He smiled at the Norseman. "Sir Bjorn?"

"Ja?"

"Lord Yves requires your attendance." He pointed toward their host lest the man not understand some part of what he said.

"Ja!"

Up Sir Bjorn stood, towering above the table. Down he strode to Lord Yves's chair. Zander watched him address their host. Lord Yves bent forward and cast a dark look toward Zander, then turned and pointed in Hugo's direction.

Zander turned his body toward Elinor. "Your father fell asleep, and Lord Yves has decided to have him brought home."

"Surely, he can just walk with me."

"It isn't clear how much wine he drank, so better to have men do it in case he needs more support than you can give. Besides, this way you can stay."

She made movements to get up. "I really should—"

"He needs his pallet, not a mother. Stay. I am told that the cook made a special almond cake. The castle folk have been drooling in anticipation all day and talking about little else."

She hesitated. "Almond cake, you say?"

"Lots of butter, they said. And honey, I think. Does that sound right? I don't make cakes myself."

"It sounds just right. Perfect." She licked her lips in a way that sent his mind in the devil's direction. "I suppose I can stay a while longer."

Zander poured her more wine.

***

"I must go now." Elinor licked the remnants of her second piece of almond cake off her fingers. For some reason Zander stared as she did so.

"Why?" He pulled his attention away from her fingers. "I will make sure that you return safely, and it is not very late. Why not see the castle while there is still light outside?"

"Could I?"

"Of course." He pushed back his chair. The meal was done, and the boards were being removed so dancing could start. "Come with me, and I'll show you the chambers above, and the grounds."

Zander appeared at home in Lord Yves's castle, but then he had been here some days now. Still, it impressed Elinor how he guided her to the stairway as if he owned the manor, and handed her up the stairs.

"Are you sure this is permitted by Lord Yves?" she asked while she mounted the stairs and felt him behind her. "He gave you a very odd look while we passed him."

"That was only an acknowledgment from him. A way of saying 'Go right ahead, my home is your home.'"

It had looked more like a warning, and a way of saying "Watch your step and where you trod, Sir Alexander."

All the same, eager to see the castle's appointments, she followed Zander's lead through the chamber where her father had recently spoken to Lord Yves, to another room that looked to be arranged for family doings. Only little in it spoke of family. Some books and furniture kept it from being barren, but it possessed a spare, unused look.

"Has he no wife or children?"

"His wife passed away years ago. He has a son who is being fostered now, with a lord in the south."

"I suppose he will remarry some day."

"He says he prefers widows with lots of land. If he finds one, he will probably marry her."

"Maybe he will marry Lady Judith."

"He has indicated not. He doesn't like her nose."

She laughed. "She looks to be very wealthy. What difference does a nose make?"

"He says it is very important. Although, perhaps he also finds her too. . . voracious."

She stopped to admire a very nice chair in the second room. "She did seem to have a strong appetite, so perhaps he is right in that. Although it is an odd thing to hold against her, especially since he can afford whatever amount she eats."

She turned away from the chair to see Zander watching her with a bemused expression.

He opened another door. "Come in here. It is the finest solar I have ever seen."

She stepped through to a chamber flooded with the red light of the setting sun. A very large window, one made up of many small pieces of glass held together with lead tracery, faced the west. She smoothed her fingers down the glazing.

"This must have cost two fortunes."

"At least," Zander said. "It would be pleasant on a winter day to sit in this solar, out of the elements but with views of the countryside." He came up beside her. "Watch this." He pushed a lever on a central panel of the window and swung it back, leaving a large hole open to the air.

She peered out. "An army could come through this entry. What if the castle is besieged?"

"That is a private garden below, and a good wall around it. Any enemy would have to breach three walls to get to this part of the castle, and that would be after they entered the town to start."

The little garden below appeared quite lovely. A little spot of paradise. "There are flowers down there."

"There are more beyond its wall in the main garden. Would you like to see it?"

"Oh, yes. After days with few trees and too much dried grass, some greenery and flowers would be wonderful."

"Let us go while there is still light." He closed the solar window, then took her hand and guided her back through the chambers to the stairs. Down they went, this way and that. Zander had come to know this castle very well.

"Are your lord and Lord Yves friendly?"

"Friendly enough, although I don't think anyone knows Lord Yves's mind enough to think of him as a friend. Why do you ask?"

"I wondered why he would allow you to learn his castle so well. If you can move so freely, you have probably studied its defenses and now know its vulnerabilities."

"I would never violate his hospitality thus."

"You assessed what it would take to gain entry through that solar."

He opened a heavy oak door. "It is a natural reaction. We all are always thinking about war strategies."

The door gave out to a garden that stretched from the castle proper to the wall that enclosed it. Bathed now in the evening's light, gold washed the leaves and rose tinted the stones. A pear tree grew in the center to give shade in the afternoon, and shrubbery lined two paths that crossed, intersecting in the middle. Even in winter this would be a special place.

A fragrance drifted on the light breeze. She ventured down the center path toward the colors visible behind the shrubbery, in the back northern corner. A bed of flowers thrived here, with a cherry tree standing sentry against the wall.

She bent down and stuck her nose to some white roses, gleaming pink now in the setting sun's last light. Their aroma intoxicated her.

She straightened, heady with the scent. The light had dimmed, and dusk's gray light spread. "I should return to my camp."

"No."

She turned, surprised. Zander stood two arm spans away. He had been watching her revel in the flowers' fragrance. Now the fading light cast his visage into the angles of a stone sculpture. He might be one, the way he towered there, tall and straight.

Except for his eyes. They were alive and full of lights that reflected his spirit. They now showed deep consideration.

"I should not dally," she said, thinking that "No" presumptuous.

"He is sleeping off the wine. You can stay longer."

"It grows dark. Soon the flowers will not be visible anyway."

"Except one." He took her hand and led her toward the wall. She did not go willingly but did not resist either. She would see this flower, then have him take her to her tent.

He stopped near the wall. She looked around. "I see no flower here."

"I do." He stepped closer. So close, she had to bend her neck to look up at his face.

Such a face it was. She had known him so long that she often forgot his beauty but now it looked down at her, his expression oddly stern and his mouth in a firm line. Stars brightened his eyes, but behind them, she saw a hunger. She understood suddenly what had been meant by Lady Judith being voracious. The men did not speak of ordinary hunger but of desire.

That was what she faced now, so obviously that she knew she should walk away quickly. Instead, his gaze mesmerized her, and enlivening thrills twirled inside her and caused her core to quicken.

It did not surprise her when he embraced her and pulled her close. His head dipped, and he kissed her hard, and she was in a spring garden not a summer one, and allowing the excitement of a young man's want of her.

All evening, throughout the meal, the devil had worked his dark magic on Zander's mind. He'd watched that Norse clumsily flatter Elinor, and heard her musical laughter. He noticed how older knights and lords watched her too. She had no dowry but that would matter not to some of them. Whether as wife or leman, there was a good chance she would be claimed before the week was out. Her beauty was so distinctive it caused men to look twice, and to wonder what removing her gown would reveal.

He could not stop that. Her father would take any settlement offered, in order to see her secure. Hugo might demand nothing at all for himself. The notion, once planted in Zander's head, maddened his thoughts and left him angry and raw because there was one man her father would never countenance in any way, and that was Sir Alexander de Mandeville.

As soon as Sir Hugo issued his challenge, she would not have him either. A woman does not kiss the knight who might kill her father.

Claim her while you can. Bury yourself in her body so you are each a part of the other forever, and she never forgets you.

It was not a thought worthy of a knight. He didn't care. His desire had only grown since he first saw her in that tent while he studied the woman's things near the one pallet, and realized she was at the tournament. She plagued his dreams now, and he had already taken her, many times, in his mind. It was tonight or never, as he saw it, and never was unacceptable.

He pulled her closer yet, so her breasts pressed against him. He consumed what he could, using his mouth to kiss and bite her jaw and neck before kissing her soft lips again. He pried her mouth open with his tongue, then explored within. She startled a moment before permitting it.

Her arms rose to embrace him. He noticed how she took care not to touch the wound on his arm. Her gesture of acceptance cut the one thread still existing to his conscience. Once his desire tasted the first sign of victory, it ruled him.

If not now, never.

He caressed her breast softly, deliberately, his goal to give her such pleasure that her own conscience went silent. She inhaled with a magical note of wonder at his touch. He continued while her breaths shortened and those notes sounded, again and again, merging into low, quiet cries of joy.

One bird sang as night fell, then quieted. No sounds came from the garden now. He continued caressing her while his other hand worked at the lacing to her gown.

She did not react, if she even noticed. Her own kisses distracted him and slowed his progress. Soon, however, the gown loosened, and he eased it down. More touches through the linen of her chemise, then he lowered that as well.

Some starlight illuminated a bed of ivy near the wall, much like dawn might break the night. He backed up to that green coverlet so he could see her. No kisses now, only careful strokes over the snowy white of her skin while he admired her astonishing beauty.

She looked down at what he was doing. If she denied him, it would be now. He waited but continued pleasuring her with his hand to tilt the scales in his favor.

When she did not stop him, did not object, he laid her down.

Unearthly pleasure. Astonishing sensations. The ivy tickled her cheek but she barely noticed. Zander's hand raised devilish desire in her, and overwhelming need. She hoped it never stopped but worried she might die if it didn't.

He lay beside her, his hand moving high and low, down to her belly, then up her legs beneath her skirt. She felt the night air on her legs and breasts. Her mound itched with a strange impatience. So this was what Lady Judith craved. Small wonder.

A thought slid through her euphoria, that Zander had done this with other women. She knew neither jealousy nor suspicion. She was beyond judgements such as that. She only wanted to live in this little world with him, where she smelled that vague sandalwood on his garments and his breath warmed her skin and nothing else, nothing at all, mattered except the profound closeness she felt with his body and soul.

His head dipped. His dark hair feathered against her face. A new pleasure, sharp and insistent, flowed through her. She realized he used his mouth on her breast now. It was the last clear thought she had.

Sensations too amazing to handle piled up then. Licks on her breasts and caresses on her legs. His hand on her mound sent her to the stars. Touches down there, first gentle then less so, brought her close to screaming.

Then he was in her arms, on top of her, his hips settled between her thighs. "I know you are a maid, Elinor. If you do not fight it, it will not hurt much."

She knew when he started. A fullness pressed, then continued. Her body did rebel, and he paused. She looked above to the stars. He lifted one of her legs over his hip and pressed again. The tear of her maidenhead made her gasp, but after that she only felt that fullness stretching her more and more.

He stopped, his weight resting on his forearms so he did not crush her, his head bent so he could see her face beneath his chest. He dipped his head down and kissed her. The intimacy of this joining, of two bodies made one, overwhelmed her.

"Kiss me again, Zander," she whispered.

He did while he pulsed inside her. Then he moved, so the joining became a living action. She gripped him tightly. It didn't hurt much, but it still hurt. Yet his spirit and care and arms surrounded her, and she savored every moment.

When it was done, and he laid atop her, his breaths short and deep, his hair hanging onto her face and his eyes closed, she branded her mind with the beauty of his face in this expression of spent passion, and the sensation of him still in her.

"Don't leave yet," he said after he had fixed her gown and his own garments. "Lie with me a while."

Elinor had not said anything about leaving, but he knew her mind was going in that direction.

"I heard the curfew bell."

"Do not worry. I will get you out."

He gathered her in his arms and laid in the ivy with her warming his side.

"Did I hurt you?" He had said he wouldn't much, but he really had no experience with knowing about that. Knights did not take maids who were not their brides. It wasn't done, but then again, it was sometimes, as he had just proven. One more example of how knightly honor was little more than fine words. It was his first time for doing it, though, and his reassurance had been a hopeful lie.

"Some. Not too much," she murmured, turning toward him so their faces rested closely. "I am glad we did this, Zander. I am glad it was you."

At the moment he did not seek absolution, but he thought it sweet she gave it anyway. He was too contented to have any worries, least of all

69

those about sin and retribution. He'd had many women, but had never been this moved by it. He had known more than pleasure with Elinor, and he did not think he would ever regret following his darker inclinations.

"You left Sir Morris as a squire," she said. "When were you knighted?"

"While fighting for King Henry."

"So then, after Henry died, and Richard finally followed his vow to go on Crusade, you went with him as my father did. It was why you had joined that little band going to France to begin with."

"It took a long time to get there, what with his coronation, then his raising the funds to pay for his army. I thought we would never leave France. Eventually, we did, sailing first to Sicily, then to Cyprus. We took Cyprus before finally going to Acre."

"Which he conquered. There was much rejoicing here when word finally came. Was it glorious?"

He supposed people did think it glorious to win battles, especially ones like that. But talk of this had dimmed his joy in having her, because she did not understand what that Crusade had taken from him.

"There isn't much glory in war, Elinor." He caressed her face, stroking some damp locks off her brow. "It is a black moment when you kill your first man. It matters not what his religion or birth was. It becomes easier with time. For some men, too easy."

She gazed at him as if she pondered his words. "If it did not become easier, there could be no wars."

"That's the truth of it." Being a woman, she probably thought that preferable. There were times when he did too.

"Is that why you left? Because it had become too easy?"

He looked at her, surprised. How like Elinor to see more than anyone else.

"Forgive me," she said. "But. . . you said the years had changed you, and they have. Not all the time. But there are moments when you appear far away in your thoughts, and quite old."

His soul churned. Her words conjured memories that he did not welcome. They came at night sometimes, in dreams, when he had no control over his mind.

"I left because killing had become too easy and still not easy enough for the king's purposes."

She rose up on one arm and looked down at him. He felt her gaze searching his face as if she could read the truth there without asking for it in words.

He pulled her back down into his arms. "After the victory at Acre, Richard and Saladin, the Saracen leader, made a truce. An exchange of prisoners was part of it. Saladin handing over the True Cross was another part. There were other things too. A date was set for it to take effect. Only neither one wanted to release his prisoners first."

"They didn't trust each other to complete the exchange."

"They did not. Neither trusted the other to uphold the treaty."

"Who finally went first?"

"Neither." He gritted his teeth against the anger that wanted to burst in him. "Richard is a great warrior. He is impulsive, however. And he does not think ahead the way a king must. So there he was, getting angry, and also impatient to march on to Jerusalem. He decided to break the treaty for good. Only now, he had almost three thousand prisoners."

"Did he free them and get nothing in return?"

"No." He gazed up at the sky, the stars bright now and the moon low. He did not speak of this. Other men did, but not him.

She was not to be denied the end of the story. "What did he do?"

"He killed them. Or, we did. On a nearby hill called Ayyadieh. He had them all brought there and put to the sword."

He heard her sharp intake of breath. He waited for her to pull away, out of his arms.

Instead, she caressed his face. "Your king commanded it. You had no choice."

"Do not make excuses, Elinor. I don't." He sighed so deeply that he felt his soul left him on his breath. "The enemy's army was below the hill, shouting curses at us. I was on the line holding them off when they tried to attack. Then I looked back and saw—It was not only enemy warriors dying. There were women and children."

She buried her face in his shoulder and clutched him hard. "What did you do?"

He remembered that moment, when he faced the carnage. In that instant nothing he believed held true anymore. There were some who had enjoyed the killing, but others who were repulsed by their own actions on that hill. He'd even seen two knights approach Richard to argue against the deed, only to be rebuffed.

"I could not stay there. I had not gone with the king to kill unarmed men and women and children. The way back into the city was blocked. So I walked down that hill. I assumed I would be killed." He almost said he had counted on it. Nor would it have mattered. He was already dead inside, or at least all that was good had seemed gone.

"Yet you weren't killed."

"As I was leaving my position, a woman broke through our line, trying to escape. She was right near me when she was caught. Two men began to drag her back. She had two children with her. She looked at me with such fear—" A weak word, fear. It did not describe what he saw in her eyes. "I pushed the men away, grabbed her arm, and threw one child on my back. Then I started down. I sheathed my sword. It would do me no good. When I approached the enemy, I released the woman and she and her children ran to the army." Sometimes he relived that slow minute while he paced forward.

"Did they spare you because of that woman?"

"I assume so. They let me pass. I kept walking until I reached the port. I did not march to Jerusalem with Richard. I did not want to look at the man again, let alone serve him with my sword."

She held him in silence, occasionally giving him a kiss of reassurance. Then she turned on her back and looked at the sky with him.

She bit her lower lip. "Who will you fight for if there is a war between the king and Prince John, if Richard so disappointed you?"

"There will be no war, Elinor."

"I wonder."

He shifted so he could see her face, and her puckered brow. "There are those who plot, and John hopes enough do. He would be an usurper, however. There are men here, recruiting others to his cause. I hope they have not influenced good men to take risks that are treasonous."

She wiped her eye with her hand and he realized tears had formed. "Such a frightening word, treason. I worry about my father, Zander. He is making friends who I do not think really care for him, but only seek to use him."

He soothed her with a kiss. "Speak reason to him, so he does not get drawn in too deeply."

"If men listened to women's reason, there would be no treason, no wars, no uncompromising honor. Alas, we are ignored."

"I will never ignore you if you speak reason to me, darling."

She wrapped her arm around his neck, kissed him, then buried her face against him and inhaled deeply. "I must go. You know I must."

"I will take you back now."

They stood, and she brushed off her skirt. Then she placed her hand on his chest. "I am honored that you told me about that day, Zander. I think you believe it has left you bereft of your own goodness, though. It has not. You are not really The Devil's Blade. You are the same Zander, deep inside."

He guided her through the quiet castle. All the guests had retired, although Lord Yves probably entertained a few in those private chambers near the solar. In the hall bodies stretched on pallets laid on the floor. Some slept on benches.

Out through the town they went. He knew all the guards at the gates, and he gave the one on duty now a coin so they could both pass. He brought Elinor as close to her camp as she would permit and watched carefully while she walked the rest of the way.

No sooner had she entered her tent, then another figure emerged from one of the others. The man walked toward Zander, avoiding the light from any fires. Zander saw it was Sir Lionel.

He followed at some distance, surprised to see Sir Lionel aiming for the town gate. With the curfew he should not be able to enter, yet he did so easily. Either he had bribed the guard, or someone in the castle had arranged for his entry.

As a castle guest, Zander followed him into the town. Lionel kept walking with purpose until he passed through the castle gate itself.

Zander followed. Lionel began mounting the stone stairs in the keep. Zander pressed against the wall at the first curve and listened. Lionel kept climbing until he reached the highest level. The only chambers up there were Lord Yves's and those of his most honored guests. Lionel's progress changed from boots on stairs to boots on passage. Zander counted the steps before the sounds disappeared.

He went up there too, to judge which door Lionel had entered. He guessed the one at the end.

He turned to go when Lord Yves's own door opened, and Lord Yves looked out. "What are you doing up here?"

Zander thought fast. "I was seeking a certain widow with an unattractive nose."

"You are close, but Lord Marcus will be displeased if you steal into his chamber and try to tup his wife." He pointed in the other direction, toward the stairs. "The woman you seek is behind that last door."

Zander made what he hoped looked like the smile of a randy knight glad for the help. He moved down to the door in question. He looked back. Lord Yves still watched.

Cursing under his breath, he scratched on the door. It opened and Lady Judith peered out, surprised. Then she grabbed him by the tunic and hauled him inside. Knowing it would take all of his wits to avoid being devoured, he set aside for the moment considerations of why Sir Lionel was secretly meeting with Lord Marcus, and whether Lord Yves knew about it.

Elinor lifted a water bladder as quietly as possible. She grabbed some rags and ducked though the flap, out into the night again. Taking a basin from near the embers of the hearth, she carried everything to the back of the tent and set about pouring water into the basin. She lifted her skirt, wet the cloth, and began cleaning the blood off her thighs.

The night afforded some privacy, but it would not do to cleanse herself in the morning anyway. Her father had retired early so he would rise with the sun and she did not want him speculating on why she needed to wash this thoroughly.

She could not see but she could feel the dried blood and Zander's seed and scrubbed as best she could. A visit to the reeds and a full bathing was probably in order. She would have to find some washerwomen to join so she did not go alone again.

Her memories of the garden still filled her head. Details had emerged while she walked back, and she suspected her conclusion had been correct and that Zander had spilled his seed outside of her. That might help prevent her from getting with child—a consequence she had considered not at all when she was giving herself to him.

A quiet joy persisted in her heart. She did not regret what she had done. Should her father force her to marry Sir Gerwant, or some other man, she at least had for once given herself to a man who mattered to her. The intimacy of their joining still filled her, made all the more intense by his confidences about his crusade.

"What are you doing, daughter?"

Her father's voice caught her up short. He had slept off the worst of his drink, it seemed. She steadied her heart and continued her task. "Washing."

"Why would you be doing that now?"

She thought fast. "I have my flux."

"I saw no rags."

"I just got it while at the supper. That is why I need to wash. It is all over my legs." Such lies thieves told when they were caught with their fingers in the wrong purse.

She felt him watching her.

"I trust you have not been playing the whore."

She pretended she did not understand what he was really asking. "If I were, we would be eating better. Become suspicious when I serve you beef or pork, not when you are eating soup."

He crossed his arms, not leaving.

"Please turn away," she scolded. "Leave me my modesty, at least."

He turned and looked out to the north. "If we are invited again to the castle for a meal, I will ask Lord Yves to sit you beside me. I saw Sir Alexander on your right again. I'll not have the man feeding you lies."

"He fed me nothing." Except an incredible morsel of swan once. "He barely spoke to me. All of his attention was on Lady Judith. She is a wealthy widow with rich lands."

For some reason, that annoyed him. "You were the loveliest lady there, and all could see it. Rich lands are not everything."

Actually, they were. Elinor would cherish tonight forever, but she had no illusions about Zander. He would marry a woman with a dowry that would establish him in ways Elinor of York could not. Either Lady Judith or one of those girls brought here to find a husband.

"All the same, I don't want him near you."

"Do what you will. It matters not to me where I sit. Now leave me. I must finish here so I can sleep in comfort."

He hesitated, then walked around the tent.

Eight

His dream shook. No, not his dream. The real world. He opened one eye to see a young page at his bedside, grasping his shoulder.

"What do you want?"

"My lord requires your attendance in the solar."

Zander told him to leave, then swung his legs so he sat on the bed's edge. He wondered if Lord Yves had learned about Elinor and was going to get paternal or priestly about it. More likely, he had noticed Lady Judith's discontent this morning and wanted to advise him to grab those lands while he could.

He had left the lady in the early hours, after much laughter and dodging on his part and bawdy innuendoes on hers. He did not think his resistance had discouraged her. Rather the opposite. If he wanted marriage and those lands, he could not have devised a better plan. She'd concluded he was saying, in not so many words, "If you want me, you will have to marry me."

He dressed and began mounting the stairs to the solar. He would have to go out to the camp after this and prepare for a challenge this morning. He also needed to tell Angus to do a few things for him.

A page escorted him into the solar. The big window was open, permitting a fresh breeze to flow. Lord Yves sat in a fine chair in front of them. Standing to the side was Sir Hugo.

"Join us, Sir Alexander," Lord Yves said. "I've a decision to make, and you should be here when I do."

Zander advanced until he stood in front of Lord Yves.

His host pointed to his left. "Sir Hugo has come to request a challenge against you."

"He had only to go to my camp and tell my squire."

"It is not that simple. I must approve certain challenges for personal combat. Those *à l'outrance*, for example, which is what he demands."

Zander turned on Sir Hugo. "This is madness."

"I'll let God decide that."

"Men favored by God die in battle all the time. It is the same at tournaments." He turned back to Lord Yves. "You must refuse him this request."

Lord Yves made a steeple out of his fingers, with the tips on his mouth. He thought about that. "He has a strong argument with you. I cannot ignore his accusations."

He repeated what Sir Hugo had said, while Sir Hugo stood there glowering. Zander had heard it all before and was tired of the lies.

"Tell him the truth, Sir Hugo. That was not how it happened, and you know it."

"It is. Do you now also insult me by saying I am lying?"

"Not lying. Just being forgetful."

"My memory is good enough to remember treachery such as yours."

Zander turned to Lord Yves. "We were getting him out. I was helping him. Then he broke away and ran back. We had passed a group of fallen Saracens and some had helmets and swords decorated in gold. He wanted the spoils and left us in order to collect them."

Sir Hugo's face reddened. "Lies!"

Zander ignored him. "It is the truth, I swear to you."

Sir Hugo grew agitated. He looked worried. "There is more that I did not say before. A new cause."

"What is that?" Lord Yves asked.

"I have good reason to believe he has dishonored my daughter, and thereby me and my family."

Zander gritted his teeth. The devil take the man. He had just ruined his own daughter for the chance to fight this combat.

Lord Yves's heavily lidded gaze swung slowly to Zander. He looked right into Zander's eyes. Zander returned a steady gaze of his own, but he doubted Lord Yves concluded he was innocent.

Lord Yves turned to Sir Hugo. "You witnessed this?"

"No, but—"

"Others did?"

Hugo shook his head.

"I have decreed that the reason for combat *à l'outrance* must be announced. I will not have a woman's name stained on nothing more than a father's suspicions. That cause is rejected."

Hugo huffed and frowned and got red again.

"As for the other, you each have a story and I am not the man to choose which is true. I will permit the combat *à l'outrance* on that cause, Sir Hugo."

Beaming with satisfaction, Sir Hugo left the solar. Zander glared at Lord Yves. "You as good as signed a death warrant. He is unable to compete."

"You mean that leg? He won't be using it much."

"It isn't just that."

"Ah, you assume his age will defeat him. You think he is too old."

Far too old. Zander swallowed the response. Lord Yves was of similar age to Sir Hugo. His host probably would not take well to arguments that knights lost their prowess once they passed five and thirty.

"There is one other combat *à l'outrance* so far. They will all take place late this afternoon after the other combats are done. The priest will come to you before they start."

Zander stormed from the solar. Now he had to figure out how to win, but still not kill his opponent in a fight to the death.

"You've an ugly scowl on your face," Angus observed as soon as Zander entered his tent on the field.

"I've got an uglier one in my soul." He wanted to kick something, like the useless Harold, who still lay asleep on his pallet. He resorted to a firm nudge instead. "Get up. Take the bladders and fill them with water. Then go to the paddock and groom my destrier."

Harold ran out, watching as he passed for a blow that might be coming.

Zander crossed his arms, still furious.

"What happened?" Angus asked.

"That fool Sir Hugo asked for combat *à l'outrance*."

"Is he looking to die? Some knights when they get older—"

"I think he believes he can win."

"Unlikely."

"Unlikely? *Impossible*."

Angus tilted his head. "No need to tempt fate by saying impossible. Unlikely is good enough. Makes me sad for the woman who was here when you were wounded. His daughter, wasn't it? What will become of her if he dies?"

"I will take care of her." It came out too fast, too sure. Angus gave him a quizzical look. "Not that she will allow it if I kill her father. That is very unlikely."

"Impossible." Angus smiled as he threw the word back.

"Only heaven knows when Hugo last practiced at arms. When he was younger he was a fine warrior. Even when I became a squire. Now, besides his bad leg and vision, maybe even his sword arm is weak. I am going to tell the priest that and ask him to remind Hugo that taking one's own life is a serious sin."

"He's not planning on doing that. He's planning on killing you. You and I both know he will die, but that's not the same as falling on his sword."

No, it wasn't. Damn. Damn, damn, damn.

He strode over to where the Scot's arms lay. He lifted the shoulder plate. "Can this engraving be removed by the forge?"

"Shouldn't take long. Why would you want to do that? The decoration makes it much more valuable."

He wanted to do that so it would not be recognizable.

* * *

Elinor folded the silk veil into a little pile. Almost weightless, it did not take up much space. Nor did it wrinkle, she had learned while she sewed it. Small wonder that silk was prized.

She had seen her father return from somewhere early in the morning, as soon as she had risen. Now he had gone to watch the combats again. She tidied up the tent and began planning how to pack everything for the journey back home. She would be glad to get him away from here, and from those men who had plans she dared not name.

She wondered if her father had already found a cart to take them. If not, she must do that soon, or there would be none left.

The flap opened. Zander entered. The flames in his eyes made her pause, but he came over and gave her a kiss, then called for Angus to join him. "Where are your father's arms, Elinor?"

"Over here." She showed them the chest.

Angus threw it open. Piece by piece, he removed it, eyeing each one. He made two stacks on the ground.

"This here is fine. This group here has some rusted links and others that are broken."

Zander looked down at it. Then he crouched by the chest and poked through it. He stood.

"Bring it in, Angus."

Angus left and returned with pieces of armor. Zander took them and laid them down next to the chest. "Tell him a knight left it. Tell him you don't know the knight's name."

She looked at that plate. "Why does it matter? Has he challenged someone?"

Zander just looked at her.

Her heart sank. "Oh, heavens." He had gone and done it after all. She had hoped as the week passed and he did not fight that he would never fight anyone, let alone Zander.

"I'll not have him meet me unprepared. Angus will take the mail to the forge to be repaired, then bring it back. Do not let your father's pride prevent him from arming himself well, Elinor. Tell him that the knight said he wanted to see John's supporters triumph on the field.

Then he may not see the plate as charity."

She could barely breathe. She waited for Angus to leave with the mail, then said "My father is in no condition—"

"I do not get to decide if the knights I meet are fit for it, unfortunately."

"Don't you? You can refuse, can you not?"

"I have agreed to take all challenges. To refuse his would be cowardly. Should I prove what he accused me of at that dinner is true?"

"Everyone knows you are no coward."

"Only because I do not refuse challenges," he said firmly. "Do not pretend you do not know how it is, Elinor."

She knew how it was. Already worry sickened her, and it would only get worse. "When?"

"Late afternoon. It will be among the last of the day." He embraced her.

She hugged him hard and buried her face in his tunic. "Can you defeat him without hurting him? As you did that Scot?" She saw that combat again, and Zander wielding his sword for over an hour until he brought that Scot down even after being wounded and having no shield. Surely, such a knight could humble her father without bloodshed or sad humiliation.

When he did not answer, she lifted her head and looked at him. She saw beauty and anger, and determination and. . . sadness. "What are you not telling me?"

He kissed her gently, then took her face in his hands and looked at her. "Your father went to Lord Yves and demanded personal combat with me, *à l'outrance*. Lord Yves has permitted it."

Tears welled at the word. To the death. That combat would be horrible, and tragic for her no matter how it ended. One of the men she loved was supposed to die at the hands of the other.

"I will not allow him to do this."

"Stop it if you can, darling. I urged Lord Yves to refuse. Since he did not—"

It would happen. Today. By dusk, she would be in mourning.

"I must go," he said, setting her away from him.

82

"Will I see you before—"

"No."

She ran to her sewing and brought the veil to him. "It is done. You should have it now, in case..." She almost laughed at herself, bitterly. In case he was killed? This would never end that way. They both knew that.

He tucked the veil into his tunic and opened the flap. The midday sun fell on him, and she clearly saw the knight in him. Already he was hardening, preparing for what the day would bring.

"Zander, if at all possible. . ." She did not know the words for such a request.

He reached over and caressed her face. He turned to leave, then faced her again. "Ask him to tell you again about that day he says he was abandoned by me and the others. Maybe he will remember the truth, and not feel the need for vengeance."

His morning challenge ended fast. Angus stripped the armor and mail off him quickly once they returned to the tent. "You should eat and rest."

"I will, but now I am going to the castle."

"You think to convince Lord Yves to change his mind?"

Zander did not know what he thought. He only knew that nothing would change if he remained in this camp.

He rode his palfrey through the gate and guided it through the lanes of the town. He stopped at the mercer's where Elinor had bought her thread and purchased more steel needles for her. In the small yard in front of the church, peddlers of luxuries had set up small shacks as temporary shops. They had requested this privilege, so their expensive goods would not be vulnerable to theft out on the field.

He had seen great luxuries before, so he was not overly impressed by the wares here. Any knight who visited Saracen lands came away with memories full of gold and jewels. They were a people whose artisans created visual splendors that made even the riches of royalty in England suffer in comparison. They built their gardens to be a kind of paradise.

The items offered in these little shops were much simpler. He purchased a few things, then saw one item that impressed him. A circlet for a woman's head, made of silver. The metal had been braided before a fire had melted it all together. The silversmith showed how, with the right bale, a jewel could be slid on to dangle on the woman's forehead.

He bought it. He would give it to Elinor, no matter what happened this day. She would accept it, he assumed. If her father lived, she would see it as a gift from her lover. If her father died, she would take it as compensation for her loss. Elinor was beautiful and proud, but she was also very practical.

When he entered the Great Hall a short while later, the midday meal was underway. He ate his fill, then prepared his mind for Lord Yves. It was doubtful the lord would be swayed, but Zander believed he had to make one more effort to stop this personal combat.

He was starting to leave when another guest slid onto the bench across the board from him. Lord Marcus smiled while he broke some bread.

"I told you the money was on your being the champion. Soon now."

"It helped that two of the best jousters withdrew. Undefeated in the past, both of them."

"You are too modest."

A page brought Lord Marcus a wooden board with cheese and bread and set down some ale.

"How closely are you related to the last Earl of Essex?" Lord Marcus asked. "William de Mandeville."

"Close enough that I could not marry his daughter. Distant enough that he knew nothing about me."

Lord Marcus thought about that. "You never met him? He carried the crown at Richard's coronation."

"I was not there. I remained in France, along with most of the army."

More thinking. "If you are close enough that you could not marry his daughter, you are close enough to have a claim on his title."

"Only if someone knows how to twist the limbs on a family tree."

"There are those who do nothing else." He leaned in. "Most of them have judgments that can be influenced."

Perhaps. For a price. A large price. More than Zander expected to have, even if he pillaged this tournament for all it was worth. And if the influence depended on other than coin, he had nothing at all to offer.

The man sitting across from him did, however.

Lord Marcus looked at him. He looked back. The negotiations over this marriage had just become much more interesting.

Zander went up to the battlements. While he watched the competitions on the field, Lord Marcus's words filled his mind. It felt like a betrayal of Elinor to pay those overtures any mind at all, especially coming so soon after she'd given herself to him.

He did not feel too guilty, however. Lord Marcus had just dangled much more than land and money. There were good marriages to be had, and then there were really good marriages.

He realized he was no longer alone on the battlements. Lord Yves had arrived and watched the field just as he did. After a particularly interesting match ended, Lord Yves noticed him and walked over. "There are three strong contenders for the champion. You are one, but that last joust has made the next two competitions critical to the outcome."

Zander said nothing to that. He was not in a friendly mood toward Lord Yves today.

"Marcus spoke to you about his daughter?"

Of course Lord Yves would know. He knew everything, apparently. He probably chose his servants for their ability to hear whispers through the din of a full hall.

"Do not put too much weight on his loyalties. You only have the ones you do because of your history with Richard and your service now with Fitzwarryn. However it ends will be good enough for most of us."

"Is it so simple for you? That it matters not which brother is king and one is as good as another?"

"Since neither one will be a great king, yes."

"I suppose that is what Lord Marcus has been saying. Yet if John moves against Richard, there will be death and destruction in the realm. Good men will die for something you and he see as of no consequence. Nor will you be able to keep one foot in each camp."

"These lands are far from London and the regions where there will be fighting. Lord Jean's are too. Marcus, however, may have to choose."

"He will choose John."

"You sound very sure."

"I have reason to think so."

"You are a better spy than even I thought. What reason might this be?"

"I may be a good spy, but I am not *your* spy."

"Pity. Is this reason strong enough to refuse that dowry? You will curse yourself until the day you die if you do."

Zander knew that.

Lord Yves sighed as if the conversation had lost his interest. "By this evening you will know what to do. Lady Elinor will never have you if you are victorious and her father is killed. And if you are killed instead, well—" He shrugged.

Zander pushed away from the wall so he did not put his fist into his host's face.

Nine

Elinor filled her day with duties, but they never distracted her from what was coming. She made sure her father's crimson surcoat looked fitting for his combat and laid out his repaired mail. She placed the new armor for his shoulders and arms beside it, and cooked some fowl so he might have a decent meal to help his strength.

Then she walked through the camps, hearing whispers as she passed, knowing people already pitied her because soon she would be without her father's protection. Combats to the death were uncommon at tourneys, and no carpenters had followed the knights here to make coffins. Discouraged, she turned toward the castle and town, to see what could be found there, and to discover if a fallen knight from the tournament could be buried in the churchyard.

She trusted Zander would not require forfeit of her father's arms, not that there was much to gain from them. Still, she could sell them and perhaps pay the fee that was named for a burial. Sick at heart by how the sun moved so relentlessly through the sky, she made her way back to her camp.

She ducked inside to find her father on his pallet, with his arm slung over his forehead and his boots off. He looked to be sleeping, but he moved his arm and gazed down his body at where she stood.

"Come sit with me, Elinor, so I can see you."

She sat on the edge of his pallet, near his hip. The wound that had caused his leg pain had happened right here, a deep gash from a

Saracen's sword that broke through the mail to cut him deeply. It had healed while he was in France, but not well, and it pulled forever now.

"We'll be in the money by tonight," he said. "Once I take his armor and horses."

She closed her eyes to hold in the tears.

"Where did that other plate come from?" he asked.

"A man brought it. A knight. He said he did not want you fighting without good protection. He said you should have better if you met Zander on the field."

His gaze found her again. "Zander. You speak of him with familiarity."

"We were children together. I will always think of him by that name."

"You are not children now. I'll not have you weep for him when this is over, Elinor. He has dishonored me and must pay."

"I will not weep for him."

He seemed to accept her answer as obedience to his will.

"Father, can you not stop this? Or at least tell the lord you do not require it be to the death?"

"To turn back now would be cowardly. I'll not have men say that of me."

Something in his voice said he might have chosen differently if the decision came to him at this time.

"Perhaps Z—Sir Alexander would be willing to find a way that would not make either of you appear a coward."

"I'll not be asking such as him for favors."

"Not a favor. A mutually useful change, that is all. You can still defeat him and still take his horse and arms."

He did not speak for a while. Then he shook his head.

"Do you want me to rub the salve on your hip?"

"I already did it."

She wished he had waited for her so she could care for him one last time. "You never told me how the wound happened."

He sighed. "The Saracens have these curved swords. Damascus steel, many of them. More steel than we ever had. This horse came upon me without warning. I was lucky I kept my head. But that devil's sword swung low and caught me here. I could tell it bit through the mail."

"You were with those other knights then?"

"We were still together. Others saw me fall. But they began to fall back when an order came from Richard. They left me there."

"I have never understood why they would do that. You were one of them."

"Cowards is why. All of them, from king down to squire."

She took his hand in hers. He gripped hers tightly.

"Did no one try to help you? No one at all? That surprises me."

He fell silent.

"Father?"

"Seems one of them may have picked me up and tried to help. I don't remember it too well. That sword had stunned me, and the Saracen's horse pushed me over. Even so, it did not last, and they ran and left me there to die. That Frank found me first, and for that I am grateful since I kept my head, but he proved to be a blackguard looking only to profit off me."

It had not been a ransom as such demanded since the Frank fought on the same side as her father. The message that came said her father had promised to compensate the Frank for saving him and getting him to safety, and for passage home. Even so, it had been a large sum, and she did not think her father had named that amount in any negotiations.

"Father, is it possible that they did not leave you so much as you left them? To go back and fight? If you believed the battle was not lost, perhaps."

A silence met that question, one that was deep and hollow and full of trembling anger. Then suddenly, to her astonishment, her father began to cry.

"I might have. I see fallen Saracens, and their helmets and swords and... I may have. I was found amidst those bodies."

"Perhaps you returned and fought again and brought all of them down."

He nodded. "Quite likely."

"If so, you were not left behind. You chose to stay behind. If there is even some possibility of that, you must not fight today. You must stand down."

"What would I say? That I may have got it wrong and that maybe it was different? They will all say that I am not only lame but entering my second childhood." He sat up and shook his head. "It would not be honorable. I have challenged a man, and I will meet him. There are those expecting me to."

"Father—"

"No. Do not speak of this again." He lay back down. "Now, let me rest, but be here to help me with my hauberk."

Furious and distraught, Elinor ran out of the tent. She stumbled her way among the pavilions until she arrived at Zander's. She pushed through the flap and found him sitting on a stool, drawing absently in the dirt with a stick.

He looked up at her, and her heart broke. Longing in those eyes, and already regret.

"You should not be here, Elinor."

"Where else would I be? With my father? He admitted to me that he does not really remember what happened on that field. Even so, he will not stand down."

He returned to his aimless drawing. "He will use the plate?"

"Yes, I convinced him of that, at least."

"He does not want to be called a coward by standing down. You know how it is."

Yes, she knew how it was. And if Zander stood down, he admitted to being a coward, as her father accused him. Neither one of them would do what she wanted. She had been a fool to come here in the hopes that maybe Zander might.

The image of Zander blurred as silent tears began flowing. She wiped them away and composed herself. "Let us speak of other things while we can. I have heard the talk. Many say you will be the champion, that you have defeated all you met in the lists."

"There is one more competition with other knights that will decide it. I may as yet not win."

"I'm sure you will. Every lord in England will want you in his service then. Even Richard might again."

"I do not think I would want that. Not after Ayyadieh. His judgement—" He shook his head. "I do not want to fight with him again."

Mention of Ayyadieh had her changing the topic. "Have you gifted your lady with the veil yet? Or will you wait for the great feast?"

He stood, stretching to his full height. "It might be best to do it today, before this challenge."

He could not think he might lose, but she admired he did not assume he wouldn't, at least in her presence.

He walked to the back of the tent and bent to a chest. He turned and came to her with a cloth bundle in his hand.

He opened it to reveal the veil. With one hand, he let it fall open, then draped it over her head.

Astonished, she looked down at the silken ends fluttering below her chin. She admired the transparent silk and how the little gold threads made it glisten even in this subdued light. While she sought the words to thank him, she felt a light pressure on her head.

"You look beautiful. See?" He placed a small looking glass in her hand.

She held it up to see dark eyes and dark hair and a very pale face. Framing it all was the red veil. A circlet of silver surrounded her head, holding the veil in place.

"It was unfair to have you sew your own gift, but I knew no one here who could do it as well."

Confused, she touched the silver. "And this?"

"That is for you too. And the looking glass. Please accept them."

She knew why he gave them to her now. By day's end, she would not be able to accept them, even if she still wanted to. A woman should not accept gifts such as this from the man who killed her father, even if that man had once been her lover.

Her hand never left the silver circlet, but her other hand dropped, removing the looking glass from in front of her face. She gazed down on that little luxury.

"Thank you." Her words came out on a rasping whisper. "I wish I had a gift to give you, so you might remember me."

His fingertips stroked her cheek and his head angled so he could see her face. "You gave me a precious gift, Elinor. Nor would I ever forget you."

She ventured a glance at his face. That was a mistake. Tears began flowing uncontrollably. Tears of sorrow and worry and anger.

He pulled her into his arms and soothed her with gentle kisses on her forehead and cheek. She cried into his tunic until she lacked the strength to weep any longer. She stayed within his arms, though, branding her memory with his scent and hold, letting the moments beat by slowly. Then, finding something of herself again, she looked up at him.

He kissed her before releasing her from his embrace. She walked out of the pavilion and back to her tent to help her father prepare.

Zander watched the joust unfold. Two knights charged each other on their destriers. It could be the last competition of the tournament.

Sir Walter remained undefeated. Sir Charles had lost once, to Zander, mere hours ago. If Sir Charles won, Zander would be the champion. If Sir Walter won, there would be one more joust between him and Zander, to determine the final winner.

At the moment, Zander actually hoped for that contest, if only to delay the other one he faced this afternoon. The personal challenge from Sir Hugo of York.

He had come close to forfeiting without engaging. When he watched Elinor weep, then walk away bravely, he had wanted to badly. What did it matter if men called him a coward? Those who mattered would know the truth, and the others could go to hell.

Now he waited to learn if there would be a brief reprieve. He wore his hauberk, and Angus and Harold waited just off the lists with his plate, weapons and destrier, prepared for either eventuality.

The lances clashed. Sir Walter's balance on his horse looked precarious, but he righted himself. They turned and charged again.

When a lance connected with a breast plate, it made an unmistakable sound. The crowd gasped when they heard it. As if motion slowed, Sir Walter's body tilted back, then sideways while he fought to regain his seat. Instead, he slid out of the saddle.

Standing quickly, he withdrew his sword, inviting Sir Charles to combat. Sir Charles could have refused, and taken the win then and there, but he dismounted.

They engaged a long time, but to Zander it seemed mere moments. Finally, Sir Walter signaled his forfeit.

The crowd grew raucous with cheering and shouting. Zander realized much of the noise was aimed at him. He had been noticed standing alongside the lists, and he was now the champion. He tried to accept the accolades courteously, but his mind was on other things as he made his way to where Angus waited.

"Sir Alexander!" The sweet young voice reached his ear as he passed the lord's stand.

He looked to where Lord Marcus and his wife flanked their daughter Matilda. She waved to him her, soft face flushed and her blue eyes alight with excitement.

He had no choice except to go over to her.

"A championship," Lord Marcus said approvingly. "You will leave far richer than you came."

Between the champion's purse and the many forfeits he had taken, that was true. And yet, at the moment, he found little joy in it. Still, he accepted the congratulations.

"I hear that you have one more challenge," little Mathilda said.

"Yes, my lady. Very soon."

She reached up, unpinned her veil, and offered it. "It would please me if you wore this."

He looked at that veil. Blue, not crimson. "Do you intend to stay for that competition?"

"Of course. Everyone will be staying."

He fingered the blue veil. "Perhaps you should not witness such things."

Matilda appeared taken aback by the subtle scold. So did her mother.

Lord Marcus seemed unconcerned. "He is being chivalrous due to your feminine frailty," he explained to her.

"I am not afraid," Matilda said. "If a man dies, I am sure it will not be you, sir."

He pressed the veil back into her hand. "I am honored, my lady. However, I fear that in the next challenge it is likely to get ruined, and that would grieve me."

Her brow puckered. She looked to her mother, confused. Her mother shrugged.

"Well said, Sir Alexander," Lord Marcus said, although his gaze suggested other thoughts. "He is right Matilda. It will be stained by blood for certain."

Zander strode away, cursing himself for closing that particular door almost all the way. Then again, right now the idea of a life with Matilda struck him as long and tedious. He would never have old memories with her or share the confidences of his soul.

He found Angus and Harold. Angus began cladding his shoulders in the plate. "The crowd grows even as we do this."

"Everyone likes blood sport." Even girls not yet ten and six.

"I trust you will make quick work of this."

"Not too quick."

Angus looked at him. "A dead man doesn't care if he has been humiliated first."

"It is not a man whose pride I seek to save."

"If her father is dead, she won't care about that either."

"Probably not. But I will."

"Just so you don't forget the goal is for you *not* to be killed. Would be a hell of a thing if you played a game of parrying only for that to happen."

Zander had to smile at Angus's deep frown. "I won't forget."

He moved his arms and tested how the plate sat on his shoulders while Harold attached his schynbalds. He unsheathed his sword and swung it a few times. He could hear the marshal's voice above the noise of the crowd, explaining the stakes of the next two competitions.

He wondered if Elinor would be watching. He hoped not, but probably so.

He took his helmet from Angus. "Let us go."

***

She did not want to watch, but she followed the stragglers aiming to the lists. She had removed the veil and silver before helping her father, but now both decorated her crown. It did not mean she wanted Zander to win. She just wanted neither of them to lose.

It seemed everyone was going to attend this competition. Not only because it was one of the last two, but also because it promised blood.

She buried herself among the bodies at the edge of the crowd that had formed. She could barely see through them. She heard the marshal's announcements. Toward the end of his call, she felt a touch on her arm.

A boy stood right beside her, with his right arm extended in a gesture that pushed back the jostling bodies around him. "My lord invites you to sit on the stand with him, mistress."

She looked across the field. Lord Yves had seen her and sent his page to bring her over.

"I don't—that is, I—" She stammered out nonsense while she searched for a way to decline the invitation.

The boy smiled and urged her forward.

She hesitated, then walked with him. If she was going to be here at all, she might as well witness what happened, instead of craning her neck only to see nothing at all.

They mounted the stairs to the stand. Lord Yves stood and greeted her, and sat her beside him, making an important-looking lord move over to create a space. "You should not be alone, Lady Elinor. This trial is yours as well as theirs."

He said that as if he knew just how similar it was and how no victory would please her. She collected what poise she could and ignored the eyes aiming her way from the other honored guests.

Movement below distracted all of them. Her father rode a horse onto the field that would be his battle ground. With his helmet and armor, no one could know his age, and on a horse his bad leg was not evident. The plate that Zander had brought gave him a presence, she had to admit, and hopefully some protection. He looked to be the knight he once was.

She wondered who had given him that horse to use and whether it would make any difference.

The crowd hushed on seeing him. Then a rumble started, and grew, like a wave from the south. It washed over the whole field as everyone reacted to Zander riding forward. He wore his own colors, not the green of his lord. He did not wear his helmet yet, so his face could be clearly seen. Hard. Pale beneath his dark locks. Fire burned in his eyes. This was not her childhood friend and recent lover. It was The Devil's Blade.

Her breath caught. She looked desperately at her father again. Panic broke in her. She began to rise, to run to her father and beg him to step down and forfeit.

A firm hand on her arm stopped her. She tried to yank away but could not. Furious, she turned to Lord Yves, to demand that he release her, to scratch at his face if necessary.

He looked straight out at the combatants, not at her. "If you do it, Sir Hugo will never forgive you. Allow him to be the knight he is."

"He will be killed," she hissed.

"It is the best way for a knight to die. Fighting, and with honor."

She stared at him, hearing the words spoken and unspoken. Her gaze swung to her father. Was that the real reason for this? Because it was an honorable way to die? The eventual alternative would not be.

She settled back on the seat. She composed herself, so she would look like the lady she had been born to be. Inside her body, however, her heart pounded, and her grief waited.

Ten

Zander eyed Sir Hugo. If not for Harold, he would not have prepared his own horse. The squire had run into their camp an hour ago to say Hugo might have found a mount after all.

Now they faced each other, lances balanced against their bodies, while the crowd waited.

He glanced to the stand. Elinor sat beside Lord Yves. She gazed at neither her father nor him, but to the middle of the field, her face calm but her eyes glistening. She was wearing the crimson veil and the silver circlet.

A marshal announced the reason for the challenge, then backed off the field. Hugo lifted his lance. Zander cursed the pride that had brought them here and kicked his destrier.

Hooves pounded. Dirt flew. The point of Hugo's lance charged forward, growing larger by the instant. Zander aimed his own for Hugo's left shoulder and guided his horse with a firm hand.

His lance connected with a thud heard clearly above the shouting. He turned his horse at the end of the list and saw that Hugo was unbalanced but still astride.

They faced each other again. A clear dent showed on Hugo's shoulder plate, above the arm that held his shield. Zander looked to the stand and saw Elinor leaning forward, assessing her father.

Lances were clumsy and imprecise. If they kept at this he might well kill Hugo while trying to avoid it.

They charged again, lances in position. Zander could tell that Hugo's lance did not hold steady and his shield's position had lowered. He aimed for the same spot on the left shoulder and connected just as Hugo's lance barely missed his own horse. This time Hugo's upper body swayed back and forth. As his horse slowed, he slid onto the ground.

Zander rode to the end of the list and dismounted.

"That was fast," Angus said, taking the reins. Around them, the crowd shouted and jeered, demanding he finish it. Then suddenly the noise changed to a different kind of excitement.

Zander looked over his shoulder. Hugo had risen to his feet, and advanced on the field, sword in hand. He favored one leg. The blows had not affected his sword arm, but his shield was low on the other. He stopped right in front of the stand, waiting for Zander.

Zander muttered a curse, and strode forward, unsheathing his sword. They engaged in a clash of steel. Zander realized that he could bring Hugo down in a minute if he chose to. Instead, he parried and sparred, to push Hugo back so the end did not come right in front of Elinor. As Hugo grew tired, his shield served him less well, and he limped harder on his bad leg.

Finally, Zander slashed down on the shield, and it fell to the ground. He swung his sword at the other arm, and Hugo's blade flew away. He brought the flat of his sword hard against Hugo's leg, and Hugo dropped to his knees.

The crowd hushed. Hugo knelt there a minute, then reached up and removed his helmet to make the *coup de grâce* easier.

Zander removed his own helmet and threw it aside. The crowd began calling for the end.

"Look at me, Sir Hugo."

Hugo's chin rose and he faced Zander stoically.

"Forfeit," Zander said. "Stand down. Retract your accusations."

Hugo's gaze shifted to the crowd. "I can't. Everyone will say—"

"You will be alive, your daughter will not mourn, and I will not have to kill an old friend."

Hugo seemed to contemplate it but shook his head.

"Do you remember that day? Clearly?" Zander demanded in a fierce whisper.

"Some."

"Not enough to call me a coward, I'll warrant."

"A few details have come to me recently." He looked up with a pained expression. "I may have gotten that wrong."

"You left us and went back to *collect spoils*. You are guilty of pride and greed, but you were not in your right head, I think. And I'll not be your executioner due to either sin."

Again Hugo glanced askance at the impatient crowd. "I don't think you have a choice."

"There is always a choice." Zander lifted his sword. "I now make mine."

Elinor could not see her father well. Zander's body blocked him. She knew he was on his knees. She could hear the crowd screaming like animals for his blood.

Then Zander lifted his sword high, both hands on its hilt. He brought it down with all his strength. Her heart turned to stone, then rose to choke her of breath. The other women in the stand gasped. Silence claimed the crowd as a wave of calm eddied from the combatants toward the stand.

The worst grief burst in her. Through filmy eyes, she watched Zander bend over. Then he backed up, and her father stood, using Zander's hand for help.

She cried all the harder. The two men spoke a moment, then walked toward the stand, with Zander supporting her father, who was limping badly now. They positioned themselves in front of Lord Yves.

Zander looked their host right in the eyes. "We both forfeit."

Lord Yves stared back at him. "You can't do that. A challenge to the death only ends when someone is dead."

"We also both stand down."

"It isn't done that way. Sir Alexander, do you want to be known as the coward he called you?"

Her father straightened enough to look less pained. "About that. I retract it. That day isn't so clear in my mind, what with being wounded and barely conscious. I've had some memories come back to me that say I was not abandoned as I thought. So, I forfeit for certain, and stand down as he said." He looked over at Zander. "No need for you to as well."

"I am not blameless regarding your accusations. I was not a coward, but I should have done more to stop you. Tied you up or hit you over the head."

"Well now, I don't know about hitting me over—"

"*Enough.*" Lord Yves gazed out at the crowd, who waited for him to speak. He speared her father with a glare. "Be more careful before you ask for combat *à l'outrance*. It creates expectations. Now I am the one who has to explain this to them."

"If you do so quickly, the next challenge can start, and maybe someone will get killed in that one," Elinor suggested.

Lord Yves seemed to agree. While her father and Zander walked down the field together, Lord Yves announced that both men had stood down and Sir Hugo had admitted a mistake in his accusation. Then he signaled for the marshal to move on to the next challenge.

Elinor waited until Lord Yves stopped talking before she excused herself from his company and ran from the stand.

She caught up with her father easily on his way through the camps, now empty due to their inhabitants watching the last challenge. He led the horse by its reins but appeared relieved to see her. He leaned on her hard while he hobbled along with the war horse breathing on their necks. She guessed that bruises were rising beneath his hauberk and leg mail.

She enjoyed every step even if he didn't. Lightness entered her spirit and she could not stop smiling. What had promised to be a horrible day had instead become beautiful.

"I've succeeded in one thing at this tourney, at least, even if I have no spoils," her father said. "I've found you a husband."

"Sir Gerwant?"

"I'm very pleased with myself on that."

They walked a few more paces. "Father, I do not want to disobey you, but you need to know that I will kill myself before I marry that man."

He stopped and looked at her. She met his gaze squarely.

He shook his head. "You really are turning shrewish, daughter. I suppose I could beat you into agreement, but somehow I don't think you would stand down even then."

She noticed his leg had become very weak. She put her arm around him to help more. "There is another thing I must be shrewish about."

"More? Saints preserve me."

"Whatever Sir Gerwant and Sir Lionel have been trying to lure you into doing—"

"Nobody's been luring me. I can't be lured."

"Whatever it is, you must swear to me now you will not do it. Today's combat was enough risk for this year and next, I think."

He made a face. He began to object. Then he shook his head again. "I suppose I can miss the adventure if you insist on it."

"I do."

"Means going back to that cottage and eating more soup."

"Right now that sounds wonderful to me."

Before going to their tent he brought the horse to a tent in the nearby encampments. She helped him remove the saddle, and they left it there for a squire or groom to tend.

Elinor sat him down in their tent and began unbuckling the plate on his shoulder. While she did so, a shadow fell on them. The squire Harold stood at the tent's opening, carrying a sack.

"I was sent to serve you." He set down the sack, opened it, and removed a small bladder. "Some wine, to clear your head." He walked over, handed it to her father, and took over with the armor. "I've got a salve for your shoulder and leg, and I was told to warm water for you to wash." He looked at Elinor. "You will not be needed now, my lady."

"But I always—"

"Not needed," her father echoed. "Been a long time since a squire has served me." He took a long draw of the wine. "Be sure to clean and oil that plate, boy. And there's sand for the mail in those sacks outside."

"His name is Harold, and he is one of Zander's squires," she said.

Her father looked surprised. He glanced in the direction of the nearby camps. "Not one of—"

"He was not sent by one of your new friends, but by one of our oldest." She gestured to his thigh. "I see that blow to your leg did not affect your mail."

"He caught me wrong, with the flat of his sword, not the edge. A fortunate mistake."

"Most fortunate." She bent and kissed his head. "Enjoy being served, while I enjoy not having to bury you."

She hurried through the camps until she reached Zander's pavilion. Heart full and beating hard, she paused only to make sure the veil and circlet had not fallen askew. Then she burst into the pavilion.

And saw at once that Zander was not alone.

Lord Marcus was saying something that made Zander laugh. His wife watched approvingly. And right in front of Zander, the girl with red hair looked up with adoration in her eyes.

She halted at once, wishing she could disappear. Silence fell and everyone turned to the intruder.

"Lady Elinor," Zander said.

She looked at him, then at the girl. "I came to thank you for today," she said. "For everything." She lowered her gaze, made a small curtsy, and turned on her heel.

She walked back to her father, thinking about that family with Zander, remembering how young and pretty the daughter was. Lord Marcus and his wife appeared to have made a decision about their daughter's future. Such a marriage would be worth far more than what Zander won as champion.

What had she expected? For the champion of the tournament to be alone after his final joust? To run into his arms and have kisses far happier than their last ones? To lay on his pallet and hold him in her arms in gratitude and love?

Her father was alive. She had been honored by Zander's gifts and memories. She had given herself to the man she wanted and shared an intimacy to last a lifetime.

Only a very foolish woman would expect anything more.

Eleven

Zander cursed under his breath as he strode through the town. Dark had fallen and doors had closed, but he could hear muffled sounds and saw the dull glow of candles. He walked fast, pacing out his discontent, negotiating with his soul. Only when he emerged through the portal and onto the field did he stop his furious stride.

It was the first time he had been alone since he parted from Hugo after their competition. The first time to be with his thoughts, and to weigh all that had happened.

An offer was coming from Lord Marcus. Soon. The arrival of that family in his pavilion had all but promised one. "We will talk after the melee," Marcus had said while they walked back to the castle, with his lady and daughter a few steps behind them.

He wished Lord Marcus had not come to his tent with that child. He had been waiting for Elinor instead, and almost called her name when he saw the pavilion's flap rising. Instead she arrived later, while Lord Marcus was congratulating him on winning the championship and Matilda was eyeing him like a favorite horse.

How polite Elinor had been, despite her surprise. Gracious and elegant. His request that she stay died on his lips when she turned and hurried away, leaving him with Matilda's adoration.

That had not been the worst of it, however. Upon returning to his chamber in the castle, Lord Yves had summoned him. That long conversation had lasted until the dinner, which in turn had gone on too long.

Long enough for Lady Judith to get him alone and propose marriage.

He gazed up at the night sky. It had been a day of good fortune and new opportunities. Most of the knights encamped here would never see the like of it in their lives.

So why was his spirit so unsettled?

He walked through the camps toward the noise coming from the tavern at the back of the field. Only his legs changed direction, and he found himself on the edge of Sir Hugo's camp. The fire was down to embers and the flap of the tent was closed. Disappointment branched through him. He had hoped Elinor would be outside.

He wanted to talk to her. He needed to say that she did not owe him gratitude or anything else. It would be pleasant to be something of the squire, for a short while, before he became The Devil's Blade again, and a knight with too many decisions to make.

Elinor turned on her pallet. Her father's snores rarely bothered her, but tonight they interfered with her sleep and intruded on her thoughts.

Then something ruffled her hair. She swatted at the mouse that had thought to make a nest. It did not stop, so she swatted harder. When that did not help, she angrily grabbed for it, only to discover she grasped not a mouse, but a hand.

"Elinor." Zander's muffled whisper came from the other side of the canvas.

She glanced at her father, who still snored peacefully. She released the hand, grabbed a light mantle, and snuck out. She draped the mantle over her shift while she walked around the tent.

She found Zander stretched on the ground, his hand still under the back edge like a thief. He noticed her and scrambled to his feet. He said not a word, but took her hand and led her away, around the camps nearby, toward the river.

She should not go. She must not. Yet she hurried her steps to keep up until they reached the riverbank.

"It is a good thing you remembered where I put the pallets. You could have ended up stroking my father's head."

"His snoring told me where he lay." He looked down at her. "I am sorry there were others with me when you came. You did not have to leave. You should have stayed."

She could not stay. She did not belong there. "Have you been with Lord Marcus all this time?"

He shook his head. "Lord Yves. Before dinner, and during it."

"He honors you."

"Perhaps. I will tell you about it, and you can be my counselor." He tugged at her hands enough to encourage her to sit on the grass. He settled beside her, so close that his body warmed her side. In front of them the inky water of the river, black like the sky, showed dancing moonlight on its ripples.

"You look beautiful in the moonlight, Elinor. But then you always do."

"You were going to tell me about Lord Yves."

His arm moved up her back. "Later." He turned his body toward her and pulled her into an embrace. He kissed her cheek as if he posed a question. She already knew her answer and turned so their lips met.

It had not been snoring that kept her awake, but wistful longing and an aching heart. She had foolishly fallen in love with The Devil's Blade, the tournament champion. He could give her nothing except these secret kisses and would promise her even less. She might be nothing more but the woman who was available, but she would hold him while she could before they parted forever.

His passion rose, carrying her along in mutual pleasure. She sensed a brooding in him fall away until they shared joy and smiles along with deep kisses and physical warmth. He laid her down, and while he kissed and bit her neck and chest, he peeled away the mantle and lowered her chemise until her breasts were bare.

Such pleasure then, as he teased and aroused her with fingertips, tongue and mouth. Breathless from sensations pitching higher with each moment, she looked up at the sky, at stars that reminded her so much of the lights in his eyes.

"You are so beautiful," he murmured while he caressed her breasts.

Each pass of his palm over the tips sent new spikes of delicious excitement down her core. "Bewitching." He used his mouth again, while his hand raised the hem of her shift.

She thought he would mount her then. Instead he touched her softly, carefully, exploring her mound with his fingers. He created pleasures that crazed her until she lost hold of everything except him and the exquisite sensations. She barely swallowed cries that wanted to ring into the night. It grew more intense, more demanding, obliterating her senses to all else, until the most perfect pleasure cracked through her, bringing with it waves of astonishing, sweet release.

He took her then, while she floated in wonder. He kissed her crown as he entered, then lifted her leg over his hip so he could seat himself deeply. His thrusts made the pleasurable waves continue coursing through her. She clung to him, welcoming his hard need, reveling in the intimacy created by her love.

"Matilda is very pretty." Elinor said it simply, while they lay on the rive bank's grass under the stars. She had not dressed yet. Her head lay on his shoulder, and his hand rested on her breast.

"All young girls are pretty."

Her head tilted and he knew she looked at him. "Will there be a betrothal at the great feast?"

It was ignoble to speak of it, here, now, after what he had just done and while embracing in such peace. And yet—

"I don't know."

"Has her father spoken to you?"

"He has made the first pass with his lance, but not yet unhorsed me."

She laughed, then rose up on one arm and looked down. "Is the dowry handsome?"

"Extremely handsome. Only a fool would refuse it." Not only land and silver now. The support of Lord Marcus and his friends in pursuing a title to which he had the thinnest claim. Yet it had happened before. It was not an empty offer.

"You have never been a fool. But the father is taking his time if there is no offer yet."

"I didn't say there was no offer yet. Just not that one yet."

She drew back in surprise. "Who? Oh, I think I know. That widow? Lady Judith?"

He nodded. Also a handsome dowry, and no father to contend with. Nor was Lady Judith a girl with adoration in her eyes. She was a woman who knew the world. "I need a man with a strong sword arm and a strong back. I care not who you love. As long as you do not scorn my bed, I don't care what other bed you lie in."

She had as good as said she would not complain if he kept a leman in the castle.

He looked at Elinor. Would she accept such a life? It was the normal way such things were handled. The songs about love were not about husbands and wives.

"I do not know the lord to whom her husband owed fealty."

"Does it matter so much?"

"I would not want to find myself bound by honor to a man I do not respect. I am finding that it matters a lot to me. Lord Yves, for example. He has also made an offer of sorts. He invited me to fight with his team in the melee tomorrow, and I agreed. He also offered me service, and his dowry, if we can call it that, is also very handsome."

"No wonder you appeared to be brooding. You have a big decision to make, and each choice means a different home and a different lord, perhaps forever." She leaned down and kissed his cheek. "You will know what to do, I am sure."

"What would you do?"

She thought about that, gazing for a moment down to the river. "If I were you, I would make the choice of lord and service more important than the woman or the dowry. You do not want to find yourself at another Ayyadieh, I think."

He pulled her back into his embrace. They lay together peacefully for a long while. Then she sat up and pulled her chemise onto her shoulders and draped the mantle over her body. "I must return, and you must sleep well before the melee."

He would have stayed until daybreak, but she was right. They had to return to their tents. He stood and took her into his arms again. He lifted her chin with his fingertips, so her face was washed with moonlight. "This was not a small thing to me, Elinor. I don't want you to think that—"

"That I was the woman who was available?" She smiled as she said it.

"Yes. If I had my way, I would—"

Her fingers went to his lips, silencing him. "Please do not say it, or my heart will break. We both know what you must do, Zander. You came here to make your fortune, and you have surpassed your best hopes. All that is left is for you to decide which fortune you will accept."

They held hands while walking back. Neither of them rushed the pace but made the most of those final minutes. They talked about meaningless things and laughed about a few of them.

Finally, they approached Sir Hugo's camp. He found himself gripping her hand tighter, and his jaw hardening.

She looked down at their hands, then up at him. "I must go now. You must go too."

He released her hand. She rose on her toes and kissed him, then caressed his face. "May you have more good fortune in the melee, Zander." She slipped away, around the tent.

He strode back to the castle. He felt like an idiot, because he could not help resenting all this good fortune he was having.

Twelve

"Here's how I see it going," Angus said while he prepared Zander for the melee. "Not much will happen until the lances and horses are done. Then I see you being the target of every knight out there since they know you can pay a good ransom for any forfeit. Also, they will get fame for besting the jousting champion."

Zander let Angus talk, even though nothing new was being said. He already knew it would be a long day of hard fighting. His mind kept wanting to dwell on Elinor and last night and the wistful mood that had claimed him after they parted. Instead, he forced his attention on the upcoming competition and trusted that once it began he would again fight like the berserker they had dubbed The Devil's Blade.

"Did you learn the rest that I asked about?"

"You mean the knights on the other team sitting pretty with ransoms of forfeits? I did indeed." Angus gave five names. "You won't be alone in wanting to take them. They will be like you, fighting every man on that field."

"I know that, old friend."

"You've already done handsomely, and you are getting that prize. No need to risk too much."

"There is another fortune for the taking out there and I've got a good use for it."

Angus finished with the last shoulder plate. "You should keep that big Norseman between you and the worst of it, is how I see it.

Fortunate that the lord invited him on the team too."

Most fortunate. Zander did not plan to hide behind Sir Bjorn, but he also did not intend to venture too far away. When a man was a head taller than anyone else, he was hard to fight. More importantly, he could see more than most. That might prove useful.

Angus picked up three extra swords, an extra shield, and a battle ax. He would keep them near the refuge in case Zander needed them. "Harold is waiting with the destrier and lances," he said.

Zander checked his armor and mail. "Let us join him."

Angus walked to the tent's flap, looking at Zander over his shoulder. "You are more like your old self today. More eager for the contest than you have been the last few days."

"I've a worthy cause to fight for, Angus. That always gets my blood up the right way."

Angus laughed. "Well, if spoils aren't a good cause, I guess there isn't one."

Elinor was relieved that her father had no intention of fighting in the melee. He was in no condition to consider it, but that had hardly stopped him thus far at this tourney.

He did want to watch, however. "We will go to the battlements," he announced when the hour drew near. "Put down that sewing and come with me."

She had no choice but to go since he might need her help getting back. She would not mind seeing the melee, at least for a while. From the way her father tucked some bread into a sack, she might be there all day, however.

They walked to the town, joining a small river of people going there to buy provisions to eat during the great event. Some would crowd the edges of the field, risking the danger of the slashing swords that got too close. Others, like her father and herself, would position themselves on the town and castle walls.

Her father paused inside the gate. "We should buy some ale and food."

"Then it is good I brought some coin. The market is this way." She led him down the lane toward the center of the town.

The shops and carts were busy, and people jostled and shouted to get the vendors' attention. The bakers had kept the ovens lit, and the smell of baking bread permeated the marketplace. They found a woman selling cooked chickens and Elinor bought one while her father purchased a bladder of ale.

"What with the bread, that should last us," he said upon rejoining her. His attention shifted to a man cutting huge hunks of cheese off a wheel. "Of course, that would make sure of it."

With a laugh, Elinor bought a chunk of cheese. "I think we are done now, no?"

"It should do."

She looked up at the wall. "You think to climb up there?"

"I can do it. We'll go up that side, to the left of the castle. The view of the field will be better there."

It took time for her father to climb the stairs. They found a good position on the wall and could see the knights taking formation below. Seeing them all at once, their lances ready and their colors ablaze on their surcoats, thrilled her. The others who had taken positions near them pointed and named this knight and that.

"That over there is where any of them can go to rest, or re-arm." Her father pointed to a roped section of the field. "It is like a sanctuary."

She spotted Zander, wearing the green and gold of his border lord. Harold held his horses. She looked for Angus and found him by the sanctuary.

"There are a lot of them," she said. "So many knights."

"There is nothing like a good melee." Her father rubbed his hands together. "'Tis the best part of a tourney."

Lord Yves's team lined up across the field. In the distance another line formed as well. All of them tipped their lances in the direction of the castle. Elinor strained forward and saw Lord Yves there, along with Lord Marcus and his family and Lady Judith and the other honored guests.

His team turned their horses and faced the opponents. A marshal shouted something she could not hear. Suddenly, both lines charged, their destriers' hooves making a noise that could be heard on the wall.

An astonishing clash of lances followed, along with shouts and cries from the field. When the lines had traded places, seven knights were on the ground. A few did not stand until men ran out and assisted them off the field.

Another charge. More men fell. The knights dismounted. Then confusion erupted, and Elinor could not tell what was happening.

All around her, people shouted for this knight or that to do something, or to watch out. She barely heard her father when he spoke.

"If you are looking for Zander, find the tall Norseman. He is nearby."

Her gaze swung to the tallest knight on the field, and she found Zander fighting nearby. Already he had one opponent down.

"It looks dangerous," she murmured.

"Of course, it's dangerous," her father said after a big laugh. "There's no fun if it isn't, daughter."

She hoped it wasn't *too* dangerous. It would be stupid for Zander to get himself mortally wounded in this melee after he had secured his future and fortune earlier in the week.

That thought had her squinting hard, so she kept him in sight. Any notion of leaving this wall after a short while left her mind.

She lifted her mantle and draped her head, pulling the edge low and the sides forward to shield her face from the sun, and settled in to watch the game of war below.

Angus entered the pavilion while Zander washed the river water off. Like many others, Zander had bathed in the river to remove the worst of the dust and sweat, but he did not want to attend the feast smelling of fish either.

Angus had returned from ransoming the last of the spoils from the forfeits. "You didn't rest long," Angus said. "No more than two hours."

"I did not need more sleep, and I have something to do before the feast." He glanced at the small leather sack Angus carried. "How much?"

Angus dropped the purse into his hand. "More than you will gain from the prize. You will leave a rich man. And there are those two palfreys you said to keep if you change your mind. They will bring good sums too, and we really don't need them."

"I'm fond of them."

"As you wish."

Zander fished six marks out of the purse. He dropped them on Angus's pallet. "For you and one for Harold."

Surprise showed in Angus's eyes. "That is generous. Like most men, I can use it."

"It is generosity to Harold, who has barely earned his keep. It is gratitude to you."

Angus laid out the fine, clean, green tunic Zander would wear to the feast, then set a crockery bowl of warm water outside on a stool. He placed a highly polished metal plate and a honed blade there too. Zander sat on another stool and began shaving.

"You want me to do that?" Angus asked.

Zander shook his head. "Go to Sir Hugo. Ask him to join me in the tavern before we go to the hall for the feast. I need to make sure he doesn't plan any surprises or becomes belligerent again if he drinks too much."

"I'd think he'd be done with that, seeing as how you neglected to kill him."

Zander scraped at his beard. "I want to be certain. If he will raise a tumbler with me, all is well. If he won't, I'll know he still harbors ill will toward me."

Elinor waited impatiently, pacing outside the tent. Her father had disappeared without saying where he was going. Now it was getting late. Almost everyone had already started toward the castle.

She wore her blue dress, and the crimson veil and silver circlet. Her colors would match her father's. She did not expect cheering when they entered the Great Hall, but she hoped they would not face anything humiliating either. A man who issued a challenge to the death, then lost and lived, was not a popular person.

The nearby encampments had emptied already, the knights and their squires making an early start to the free food and ale waiting. None of those men, not even Sir Lionel, had visited her father last night or today.

Maybe he had ceased being of use to them. Had they really expected him to best Zander in that challenge? To kill The Devil's Blade? She found that hard to believe. Of course, perhaps they had not expected her father to take it so far.

She wished she could be sure that her father would honor his promise not to involve himself in any adventures regarding the royal brothers. She feared all that talk and flattery in that circle of knights had been very appealing, however. They had offered friendship, respect, and a cause. The notion of being useful again had blinded him to how they sought only to use him.

She would be happy when they left this place, and those men and their influence. She would not mind returning to the home they knew, and the people who remembered her father as the warrior he had once been.

The last of the stragglers walked past her, aiming for the dirt road up to the castle. It was time to find her father. She would start at the tavern.

She turned away from the tent, to do just that, when laughter reached her ears. Two men came toward her, angling through the camps. She recognized her father's limp and saw that his companion was Zander.

"You are late," she said when they reached her.

"We were just having a bit of ale, daughter." He looked at Zander and grinned. "She can be a bit of a scold. Not shrewish as such. Not too much, at least."

"She isn't scolding *me*," Zander said. "You are the one who is late."

"You are as well," she said. "Let us make haste. It would be a fine

115

thing if the champion were not there when the prize is given."

She set off with long strides. They followed, side by side. Her father muttered something. Both he and Zander *giggled*.

She turned on them, hands on hips. "You are drunk already."

"Not hardly," Zander said.

Her father nodded. "Not even half so."

Zander stepped around her and continued walking. "Come along, or we will be late."

She all but grabbed her father's tunic and set off again.

"We were remembering old times," her father said. "He had some clumsy moments as a squire."

"And you were reminding him of those?"

"They were funny," he said defensively.

They had to dodge through bodies to reach the castle entrance, then squeeze through more to get to the Great Hall. Already some guests sat there. The two long aisles of tables, covered with white linens, stretched up to the dais on which the lord's high table waited. Servants pointed out benches to guests, seating the more notable closest to the dais.

Elinor assumed Zander would be sent to the front, but he had disappeared as soon as they entered, lost in the sea of bodies around them. She and her father were given places in the middle of one of the long tables, which she thought generous of Lord Yves.

Ale already waited in pitchers. Her father poured some into his tumbler. He gazed around. "Very festive. The lord has spent well on this."

Festive it was indeed. Elinor took in the flaming torches on the walls, and the low fire burning in the trench that ran between the aisles. Servants still hung more pennants from the rafters, so that fluttering colors draped the space overhead. A group blocked Lord Yves's place at the high table, and she soon saw why. Someone lifted a magnificent sword with a red jewel in the hilt. That would be sword given to the champion, she assumed.

She looked again for Zander but could not find him. Then the doorway cleared for a moment and she spotted him right outside, talking to someone. A smile, a handclasp, and Zander entered. Lord Marcus walked with him.

It was done then. The choice had been made. A good choice. The right one. She would have advised he take it, even if it meant he would live far to the south, and she would certainly never see him again. Her heart knew happiness for his sake, but sorrow for her own.

She did not grieve. She had long accepted this would happen. She guessed the betrothal would be announced here tonight, and she would have to witness it.

He smiled at her when he walked past on his way to the dais. Or maybe he smiled at her father. It was hard to tell. She poured herself some of that ale. This promised to be a very long feast.

Thirteen

Zander followed the page to the high table, curious to see where he would be seated. As the tourney champion it should be near Lord Yves. There was the chance that Lord Yves would decide that the challenge with Sir Hugo had in some way disqualified him. That was not part of the competition rules, but as host and lord of the manor Yves could do whatever he wanted.

When the servant pointed to a spot two places away from Lord Yves, it was clear that no such surprise would be coming. Since he had made plans that depended on the prize, the evidence lightened his spirit.

Lord Yves took his place, with Lord Marcus to his left. Beside Marcus, little Matilda set herself down. She saw Zander and smiled.

As soon as Zander sat, a silken fabric brushed his cheek. Lady Judith was taking the place between him and Yves. He wondered what she had said to their host in order to be given this spot. From the smoldering smile she turned on Zander, he could only imagine. Then again, this could be Yves's way of punishing him for that forfeit with Sir Hugo.

Lord Yves stood. The hall slowly quieted. Lord Yves lifted the sword laid across the table in front of the elaborate, tall salt cellar that decorated his spot. "It is time to announce the champion. I am sure we were all impressed by his prowess in the lists, and his victory comes as no surprise. It is also fitting that a crusader is so—"

"Not fitting at all," a man's voice growled from the back of the chamber. "Forfeited to an old, lame knight."

Zander chose not to look to that voice or see who had so spoken. From the corner of his eye, however, he saw some heads nod.

Lord Yves did look to the voice. "You disagree with my decision? There is time for one more competition. Perhaps you would like to challenge *me*, to see whose judgement should prevail."

Total silence greeted that. Then low laughter eddied through the crowd.

Lord Yves drank from his goblet, then continued. "I name Sir Alexander de Mandeville as champion." He looked at Zander.

Zander stood and walked down to Lord Yves to receive the sword. He raised it high so everyone could see it. Cheers and board thumping erupted. His gaze found Elinor, who had stood to get a good view, and Hugo, who pounded his table.

"The coin is above," Lord Yves said. "To discourage the less angelic among us from sin. Don't forget to have me give it to you."

Zander laughed along with those who heard. As if any man would forget one hundred marks.

He carried the sword back to his place and laid it along the front of the table. Lady Judith admired the jewel set in its hilt. Then she turned greedy eyes in his direction and laid a possessive hand on his thigh under the table.

Elinor ate enough to last her a week. Lord Yves had not spared the expense on this feast, and it made the other two she had enjoyed look poor in comparison. Many dishes passed under her nose, their scents making her heady and their flavors making her swoon. She had never understood the sin of gluttony before this meal, but presumably, those most like to succumb to it were fed like this all the time.

Her father actually gave up before she did, but he had indulged too much at the start. She had taken only morsels so that she could taste it all.

"I told you coming to this tourney would be a good thing," he said while he watched her chew a bite of wild boar.

119

"I will agree now, as long as you do not complain when I serve you nothing but soup for the next month."

His gaze shifted to some dancers performing in front of the high table. "I won't complain, if that is all there is." He grinned as if he assumed that she was joking.

She wasn't. The only improvement in their fortune was her father still had that armor Zander had brought for him to use. She would try to find Angus and ask him to come and get it before they left tomorrow. Which meant the total of this adventure's benefits had been this food.

And, of course, being with Zander for a few days.

She looked at the dancers, which meant she saw him. That widow sat next to him and wore a triumphant smile. Perhaps the decision had not been Matilda after all. Lady Judith brought more, of course, and a status as lord of her manor. Zander would want the latter. Most men would, even if it meant having a wife who somehow always looked. . . hungry.

She tore her gaze away. The table across the fires had emptied, and servants were breaking down the boards and moving benches. Dancing would begin soon.

Her father reached for a honey cake. "Just one more," he said when she gave him a scolding look. "They can do this table last."

One more meant two, and another tumbler of ale. She waited impatiently for him to finish. She did not want to watch the dancing. It was time to leave this tourney and return to their regular life.

A warmth behind her. A presence she knew bending down. "Meet me outside," Zander whispered in her ear.

She looked back, to find him gone. She debated what to do.

Her father misunderstood. "Don't be waiting on me," he said. "Go and say goodbye if you want to."

She pushed her way through the hall. The night had brought mist and a brisk, cool breeze. She looked for Zander once she left the building.

Suddenly he was beside her. He took her hand and led her toward the garden. She went with him, but a strong scold formed in her mind.

She pulled her hand away once they were under the tree in the garden. The shadows of the swaying leaves caused a lively dance in the dull moonlight falling in patches around them.

"Do not think to kiss me," she said. "You are betrothed and being unfaithful to your vows should wait a little while, at least."

He leaned his back against the tree trunk. "What makes you think I am betrothed?"

"I saw you talking with Lord Marcus. If you have not yet received his agreement, you should make haste. This tourney is over and the pavilions will be struck tomorrow."

"He was telling me that his daughter had a change of heart. She thought I looked very small in the melee next to Sir Bjorn and decided a very big Norseman would suit her better."

"What a stupid child. They don't even speak the same language. One even wonders how they will manage to…" She crossed her arms, finding herself quite vexed with Matilda.

"Manage to what? Ah. You mean with him so big and her so little, how will they manage things in the marriage bed? I will show you the most likely way." He reached for her.

She stepped back. "I think you have been too clever by half if you lost that opportunity. A few smiles, and she would have been yours. Lady Judith may bring more, but you are stuck with a woman I don't think it will be pleasant to live with."

"I agree. She does not suit me."

"You have squandered both opportunities? You are the champion. You had some fame before this tourney and now you will have more. This was your best chance. Most of the knights here would sell their souls for such good fortune."

"I am not most knights, Elinor. I do not sell my soul for coin and land. Nor do I intend to squander the opportunity of this tourney."

So, there was another girl. One she had not noticed. Of course there was. Most likely two or three.

He reached down to the edge of a rose shrub and plucked two blossoms that glowed white in the night. He picked off the thorns, then tucked one behind each of her ears. "Fate brought you here, and you reminded me of a happy youth and of days when I saw good in the world, and in myself. I could never marry Matilda or Judith if I can marry you, Elinor. Will you agree to it?"

Her heartbeat slowed while she found her breath. This garden seemed an unreal place suddenly, as if she lived in a dream. Only the distant sounds of the music reminded her that she was awake, and this was real.

"You will give up too much, Zander."

"I will gain everything I need."

Oh, how she wanted to agree and to throw herself into his arms. Only it was the reckless, carefree squire offering this, not the world-wise Devil's Blade. "I bring nothing with me. Nothing at all. *Think*."

"I have thought plenty. This is no impulse. I have enough for both of us. Enough to add to the land I have. Enough to allow you to live like a lady. I love you, Elinor, as an old friend and as a new lover, and if you agree, as my wife."

"That is not why men marry."

"It is why I choose to marry."

He sounded so certain of himself. So sure that he made no mistake. Still, she dared not believe this was happening, even if she wanted to laugh and cry all at once.

"Do you think to return to your lord?"

He nodded. "Jean Fitzwarryn is a good man. Essentially good, as you said at that first feast. Strong but honest. I am not sure that Lord Yves is. And Yves wants a household knight, while Jean wants a vassal. As for Marcus, he is sure to be embroiled in whatever happens between the royal brothers. I am done selling my sword to settle other men's arguments."

She toed at the ground, trying to contain the way her heart wanted to burst. "It does seem you have thought about it a lot." Excitement built in her. "I have heard it is colder there."

"I promise to keep you warm in winter, but with you there I think it will always seem like spring." He reached toward her, offering his hand. "Will you come back with me, as my wife?"

She could no longer keep still. She took the quick steps that brought her into his embrace. "I would be honored and proud to wed you, Zander."

He enclosed her in his strong arms. His lips pressed her crown. A glorious joy filled her, one both thrilling and peaceful at the same time. The roses that she wore surrounded them with their scent.

He kissed her sweetly. "Let us marry in the morning, out on the field, with Angus and Harold and your father witnessing our vows."

A stab of sorrow pierced her happiness. "My father. . ." The thought of him cast a shadow on her joy. She pictured her father alone in that cottage. Worse, she pictured him being lured again into the intrigues surrounding the crown.

"I already asked him for your hand, while we drank together this evening."

"He agreed?"

"He said he came to the tourney to find you a husband, and I'd do as well as any other."

"High praise."

"At least it wasn't another challenge."

It helped to know that her father approved, but thinking of him still created a hollow spot low in her heart.

"It may have helped that I said he could come with us," Zander added. "I even saved a second horse from the spoils, for him to ride with us. I think he is agreeable. And this way we can keep a watch on him, so he doesn't do something that will worry you."

She looked up at him, grateful that he understood that worry and sought to spare her. "I love you already, but all the more for being generous to him, after everything he did."

"If you love me at all, I am more than repaid."

She laid her head against his chest, savoring the embrace holding her close. Sounds of the music being played in the hall trickled on the breeze.

"Let us go and dance," Zander said. "We can celebrate our betrothal, and our love, and the end of a wonderful tourney."

Hand in hand, they strolled back through the garden.

Please Enjoy this Excerpt from

By
Arrangement

by MADELINE HUNTER

One

―――――――― ⚜ ――――――――

"My name is Christiana Fitzwaryn."

They stood in a long silence broken only by the crackle of the new logs on the fire.

"You had only to send word and I would have come to you. In fact, I was told that the Queen would introduce us at the castle tomorrow," he finally said.

"I wanted to speak with you privately."

His head tilted back a bit. "Then come and sit yourself, Lady Christiana, and say what you need to say."

Three good sized chairs stood near the fire, all with backs and arms. Suppressing an instinct to bolt the room, she took the middle one. It was too big for her, and even perched on the edge her feet dangled. She felt the same way that she had last night with the Queen, like a child waiting to be chastised. She reached up and pushed down the hood of her cloak.

A movement beside her brought David de Abyndon into the chair on her left. He angled it away so that he faced her. Close here, in the glow of the fire, she could see him clearly.

Her eyes fell on expertly crafted brown high boots, and long well shaped legs in brown hose. Her gaze drifted up to a beautiful masculine hand, long fingered and traced with elegant veins, resting on the front edge of the chair's arm. The red wool pourpoint was completely unadorned of embroidery or jewels, and yet, even in the dancing light of the fire, she could tell that the fabric and workmanship were of the best quality and very expensive. She paused a moment, studying the richly carved chair on which he sat, and the birds and vines decorating it.

Finally, there was no place else to look but at his face.

Dark blue eyes the color of lapis lazuli examined her as closely as she did him. They seemed friendly enough eyes, even expressive eyes, but Christiana found it disconcerting that she could not interpret the thoughts and reactions in them. What reflected there? Amusement? Curiosity? Boredom? They were beautifully set under low arched brows and the bones around them, indeed all of the bones of his face, looked perfectly formed and regularly fitted, as if some master craftsman of great skill

had carefully chosen each one and placed it just so. A straight nose led to a straight wide mouth. Golden brown hair, full and a little shorter than this year's fashion, feathered carelessly over his temples and down his chiseled cheeks and jaw to his collar.

David de Abyndon, warden of the mercers' company and merchant of London, was a very handsome man. Almost beautiful, but a vague hardness around the eyes and mouth kept that from being so.

A shrewd scrutiny veiled his lapis eyes, and she suddenly felt very self-conscious. It had been impolite of her to examine him so obviously, but he was older and should know better than to do the same.

"Don't you want to remove your cloak? It is warm here," that quiet voice asked.

The idea of removing her cloak unaccountably horrified her. She was sure that she would feel naked without it. In fact, she pulled it a bit closer in response.

His faint smile reappeared. It made him appear amiable, but revealed nothing.

She cleared her throat. "I was told that… that you were…"

"Older."

"Aye."

"No doubt someone confused me with my dead master and partner, David Constantyn. The business was his before mine."

"No doubt."

The silence stretched. He sat there calmly, watching her. She sensed an inexplicable presence emanating from him. The air around him possessed an intensity that she couldn't define. She began to feel very uncomfortable. Then she remembered that she had come here to talk to him and that he waited patiently for her to do so.

"I need to speak with you about something very important."

"I am glad to hear it."

She glanced over, startled. "What?"

"I'm glad to hear that it is something important. I would not like to think that you traveled London's streets at night for something frivolous."

He was subtly either scolding her or teasing her. She couldn't tell which.

"I am not alone. A knight awaits in the courtyard."

"It was kind of him to indulge you."

Not teasing. Scolding.

That annoyed her enough that she collected her thoughts quickly. She was beginning to think that she did not like this man much. He made her feel very vulnerable. She sensed something proud and aloof in him too, and that annoyed her even further. She had been expecting an elderly man who would treat her with a certain deference because of their difference in degrees. There was absolutely no deference in this man.

"Master David, I have come to ask you to withdraw your offer of marriage."

He glanced to the fire, then his gaze returned to her. One lean muscular leg crossed the other and he settled comfortably back in his chair. An unreadable expression appeared in his eyes and the faint smile formed again.

"Why would I want to do that, my lady?"

He didn't seem the least bit surprised or angry. Perhaps this meeting would go as planned after all.

"Master David, I am sure that you are the good and honorable man that the King assumes. But this offer was accepted without my consent."

He looked at her impassively. "And?"

"And?" she repeated, a little stunned.

"That is an excellent reason for you to withdraw, but not me. Express your will to the King or Bishop and it is over. But your consent or lack of it is not my affair."

"It is not so simple. Perhaps amongst you people it is, but I am a ward of the King. He has spoken for me. To defy him on this…"

"The church will not marry an unwilling woman, even if a King has made the match. I, on the other hand, have given my consent and can not withdraw it. There is no reason to, as I have said."

His calm lack of reaction irked her. "Well, then, let me explain my position more clearly and perhaps you will have your reason. I do not give my consent because I am in love with another man."

Absolutely nothing changed in his face or eyes. She might have told him that she was flawed by a wart on her leg.

"No doubt an excellent reason to refuse your consent in your view, Christiana. But again, it is not my affair."

She couldn't believe his bland acceptance of this. Had he no pride? No heart? "You can not want to marry a woman who loves another," she blurted.

"I expect it happens all the time. England is full of marriages made under these circumstances. In the long run, it is not such a serious matter."

Oh dear saints. A man who believed in practical marriages. Just her luck. But then, he was a merchant.

"It may not be a serious matter amongst you people," she tried explaining, "But marriages based on love have become desired…"

"That is the second time that you have said that, my lady. Do not say it again." His voice was still quiet, his face still impassive, but a note of command echoed nonetheless.

"Said what?"

"'You people'. You have used the phrase twice now."

"I meant nothing by it."

"You meant everything by it. But we will discuss that another day."

He had flustered and distracted her with this second scolding. She sought the strand of her argument. He found it for her.

"My lady, I am sure a young girl thinks that she needs to marry the man whom she thinks that she loves. But your emotions are a short term problem. You will get over this. Marriage is a long term investment. All will work out in the end."

He spoke to her as if she were a child, and as dispassionately as if they discussed a shipment of wool! It had been a mistake to think that she could appeal to his sympathy. He was a tradesman, after all, and to his life was probably just one big ledger sheet of expenses and profits.

Well, maybe he would understand things better if he saw the potential cost to his pride.

"This is not just a short term infatuation on my part, Master David. I pledged myself to this man."

"You both privately pledged your troth?"

It could be done that way. She could lie. She desperately wanted to, and felt sorely tempted, but such a lie could have dire consequences, and very public ones, and she wasn't that brave. "Not formally," she said, hoping to leave a bit of ambiguity there.

He at least seemed moderately interested now. "Has this man offered for you?"

"His family sent him home from court before he could settle it."

"He is some boy whom his family controls?"

"A family's will may seem a minor issue for a man such as you, but he is part of a powerful family up north. One does not defy kinship so easily. Still, when he hears of this betrothal, I am sure that he will come back."

"So, Christiana, you are saying that this man said that he wanted to marry you but left without settling for you."

That seemed a rather bald way to put it.

"Aye."

He smiled again. "Ah."

She really resented that "Ah." Her annoyance made her bold. She leaned toward him, feeling her jaw harden with anger. "Master David, let me be blunt. I have given myself to this man."

Finally a reaction besides that impassive indifference. His head went back a fraction and he studied her from beneath lowered lids.

"Then be blunt, my lady. Exactly what do you mean by that?"

She threw up her hands in exasperation. "We made love together. Is that blunt enough for you? We went to bed together. In fact, we were found in bed together. Your offer was only accepted so that the Queen could hush up any scandal and keep my brother from forcing a marriage that my lover's family does not want."

She thought that she saw a flash of anger beneath those lids.

"You were discovered thus and this man left you to face it alone? Your devotion to this paragon of chivalry is impressive."

His assessment of Stephen was like a slap in her face. "How dare such as you criticize. . ."

"You are doing it again."

"Doing what?" she snapped.

"'such as you'. Twice now. Another phrase that you might avoid. For prudence sake." He paused. "Who is this man?"

"I have sworn not to tell. My brother… besides, as you have said, it is none of your affair."

He rose, uncoiling himself with an elegant movement, and went to stand by the hearth. The lines beneath the pourpoint suggested a lean, hard body. He was quite tall. Not as tall as Morvan, but taller than most. She found his presence unsettling. Merchants were supposed to be skinny or portly men in fur hats.

He gazed at the flames. "Are you with child?"

The notion astounded her. She hadn't thought of that. But perhaps the Queen had. He turned and saw her surprise.

"Do you know the signs?" he asked softly.

She shook her head.

"Have you had your flux since you were last with him?"

She blushed and nodded. In fact, it had come today.

He turned back to the fire.

She wondered what he thought about as he studied those tongues of heat. She stayed silent, letting him weigh however he valued these things, praying that she had succeeded, hoping that he indeed had a merchant's soul and would be repelled by accepting used goods.

Finally she couldn't wait any longer.

"So, you will go to the King and withdraw this offer?" she asked hopefully.

"I think not."

Her heart sank.

"Young girls make mistakes," he added.

"This was no mistake," she said forcefully. "If you do not withdraw, you will end up looking a fool. He will come for me, if not before the betrothal than after. When he comes, I will go with him."

He did not look at her, but his quiet, beautiful voice drifted over the space between them. "What makes you think that I will let you?"

"You will not be able to stop me. He is a knight, and skilled at arms…"

"There are more effective weapons in this world than steel, Christiana." He turned. "As I said earlier, you are always free to go to the Bishop and declare your lack of consent to this marriage. But I will not withdraw now."

"An honorable man would not expect me to face the King's wrath," she said bitterly.

"An honorable man would not ruin a girl at her request. If I withdraw, it will displease the King whom I have no wish to anger. At the least I will need a good reason. Should I use the one that you have given me? Should I repudiate you because you are not a virgin? It is the only way."

She dropped her eyes. The panicked desolation of the last day returned to engulf her.

She sensed a movement and then David de Abyndon stood in front of her. A strong, gentle hand lifted her chin until she looked up into his handsome face. It seemed to

her that those blue eyes read her soul and her mind and saw right into her. Even Lady Idonia's hawklike inspections had not been so thorough and successful. Nor so oddly mesmerizing.

That intensity that flowed from him surrounded her. She became very aware of his rough fingers on her chin. His thumb stretched and brushed her jaw and something tingled in her neck.

"If he comes for you before the wedding, I will step aside," he said. "I will not contest an annulment of the betrothal. But I must tell you, girl, that I know men and I do not think that he will come, although you are well worth what it would cost him."

"You do not know him."

"Nay, I do not. And I am not so old that I can't be surprised." He smiled down at her. A real smile, she realized. The first one of the evening. A wonderful smile, actually. His hand fell away. Her skin felt warm where his fingers had laid.

She stood up. "I must go. My escort will grow impatient."

He walked with her to the door. "I will come and see you in a few days."

She felt sick at heart. He was making her go through with the farce of this betrothal and it would complicate things horribly. She had no desire to play this role any more than necessary.

"Please do not. There is no point."

He turned and looked at her as he opened the door and led her to the steps. "As you wish, Christiana."

She saw Thomas's shadowy form in the courtyard, and flew to him as soon as they exited the hall. She glanced back to the doorway where David stood.

Thomas began guiding her to the portal. "Did you accomplish what you needed?"

"Aye," she lied. Thomas did not know about the betrothal. It had not been announced yet, and she had hoped that it never would be. Master David's stubbornness meant that now things were going to become very difficult. She would have to find some other way to stop this betrothal, or at least this marriage.

Thanks for reading my contribution to the *Midsummer Knights* series. I really enjoyed returning to the medieval period with this romance, and joining other authors in creating a tournament setting with jousts, knights, ladies, intrigues, and love.

If you enjoyed **Never If Not Now**, please spread the word by leaving a review on the site where you purchased your copy, or on another reader site. Thanks so much!

If you are interested in reading another of my medieval romances, or one of my Regency-set books, links to all of my books can be found on the Booklist down below. More information, excerpts, and vendor links are available on the website pages that the Booklist takes you to.

Perhaps you would like to try another book in the multi-author *Midsummer Knights* Tournament World series. The stories do not have to be read in any designated order. They all take place during the same week, concurrently.

Forbidden Warrior by Kris Kennedy

The Highlander's Lady Knight by Madeline Martin

The Highlander's Dare by Eliza Knight

The Highland Knight's Revenge by Lori Ann Bailey

My Victorious Knight by Laurel O'Donnell

An Outlaw's Honor by Terri Brisbin

Never If Not Now by Madeline Hunter

About the Author

Madeline Hunter is a critically acclaimed, bestselling author of more than thirty historical romances. She is a two-time RITA winner and seven-time finalist. Her books have been on the *NYTimes* and *Publishers Weekly* bestseller list, and 30 of them, including her first, made the *USAToday* bestseller list. She has received seven starred reviews in *Publishers Weekly*. Over six million of her books are in print, and her books have been translated into fourteen languages. Madeline is a Ph.D. in Art History, and for many years was a professor at an eastern university. Her most recent novel, *Heiress for Hire*, the first book in A Duke's Heiress trilogy, was published in May of 2020. She lives in Pennsylvania.

You can contact Madeline through her website

madelinehunter.com

and follow her on social media:

Twitter: @MadelineHunter
Facebook: @MadelineHunter
Pinterest: @archerm2003

CPSIA information can be obtained
at www.ICGtesting.com
Printed in the USA
LVHW082146030722
722688LV00026B/825

9 780997 080216